RETURN OF THE ANCIENT ONES

CONNOR WHITELEY

No part of this book may be reproduced in any form or by any electronic or mechanical means. Including information storage, and retrieval systems, without written permission from the author except for the use of brief quotations in a book review.

This book is NOT legal, professional, medical, financial or any type of official advice.

Any questions about the book, rights licensing, or to contact the author, please email connorwhiteley@connorwhiteley.net

Copyright © 2022 CONNOR WHITELEY

All rights reserved.

DEDICATION

Thank you to all my readers without you I couldn't do what I love.

CHAPTER 1

Professor Jayo loved his job. It was the best job in the world and it was days like this that made him love it even more.

Feeling the rough sandstone crumble underneath his knees as he knelt down on the hard, crumbly orange sandstone ground. Jayo smiled as he dusted away more of the stone with his handy grey metal trowel.

Jayo couldn't believe that after all these years and the decades his father had used the trowel it was still in perfect condition. Helping them all to find treasures all over the Great Human Empire.

Pure excitement filled him as he realised he was so close to finding the treasure of a lifetime and him and his team could be made famous by the discovery.

Jayo grinned at that idea. After all the bad press around him and his crazy ideas. He definitely couldn't fail to find the ancient dragon civilisation on this long-forgotten world.

Breathing in the cool morning air that smelt of damp sand and cedarwood, Jayo continued to scrape the sandstone away. He loved the way the stone crumbled as he carefully tapped and scraped it with his trowel.

Taking a moment to stretch his back and check on what his team was doing, Professor Jayo looked up. Instantly smiling as he saw his large team of ten men and ten women hunched over various parts of the sandstone ground scraping and tapping a part.

A part of him felt bad for how historical digs always changed and morphed the landscape. Even this massive plane of orange sandstone that went on for miles upon miles was almost flat when Jayo first arrived. Despite the massive mountain range in the north that he could see. It looked fun to ski down. Maybe Jayo would think about it.

Now a week later, there were lots of lumps and holes in the landscape.

But it was worth it.

Looking up at the sky, Jayo loved the feeling of the hot sun beaming down on him. Making his skin feel toasty warm but at least the cool southern hemisphere dampened its effects. He didn't want to get burnt.

Seeing a tall woman with long blond hair and wearing a large flowery hat, Jayo nodded to her as she walked up. Just seeing his best friend Saraho was brilliant. Normally whenever she walked over to him, there was about to be a big, big discovery. His stomach was filled with butterflies. This was going to be great.

As Saraho walked over, Jayo didn't know if his loose baggy trousers and black t-shirt were very appropriate for the extreme heat when they moved onto the Northern dig sites. He would have to change but at least he was comfortable for now. And he had a big discovery to find.

Hearing Saraho knelt down next to him and start brushing some of the sandstone away with her brush, Jayo smiled and asked:

"How's the other digs going?"

"Oh they're going Champion, Pet. Gordo's found some massive chunks of dirt. Peto's found even more dirt. Dig's going champion darling," Saraho said.

Jayo gave a small laugh. That's something else that he loved about his team. They had all grown up together since Play School and they all treated each other like family. They were family.

"What those scans say Pet?" Saraho asked.

Jayo nodded rapidly. "It's another two metres until we hit the object,"

Saraho bumped into Jayo and started to brush away where he was digging.

"Jayo Pet, where's our milly escort?"

Jayo kept scrapping away the sandstone with his trowel but he didn't have an answer for her. The team was given a fully stocked military escort for the trip but when Jayo had said they were going to dig. They didn't want to come. They weren't here.

If Jayo wasn't so excited about finding the dragons then he supposed he might be annoyed. But there were dragons to find!

"I don't know, Saraho,"

Then Jayo wondered if they were investigating some massive space hulk made up of hundreds of ships that had crashed into each other. Possible.

The sound of cheering made Jayo and Saraho look up and turn to see members of the team doing drinking games.

Jayo was not impressed.

He was tempted to storm over there and shout at them. But if they wanted to have a little fun, he couldn't blame them. They had been digging for ten hours each day for three days so a little break might be good.

Turning back to the sandstone, Jayo tapped the sandstone. It crumbled. Revealing something Jayo couldn't believe.

"Everyone! Jayo Pet found it!" Saraho shouted.

Jayo could only stare in disbelief as a bright glowing shard of baby blue metal shone through the sandstone. It was shaped like a scale. It was a scale.

It was a beautiful, stunning glowing blue metallic scale.

Jayo couldn't believe it. He had found a dragon or at least a part of it. This was going to be amazing. Everyone was going to get paid, be made famous and actually get out of poverty.

Which is all Jayo really wanted for his team. He knew how lucky he was by getting to live in privilege all his life, he sadly knew his team wasn't so lucky. Jayo just wanted them to be okay.

Seeing they were all around him, crouching over the amazing glowing piece of metallic scale, Jayo wanted to say something. But he was so focused on the beautiful piece of history in front of him.

Saraho hit him.

Jayo focused on his team yet he didn't look away from the scale.

"Everyone form a circle around us. We all need to dig on this spot. We need to excavate the entire dragon,"

No one moved.

"Come along now everyone. Be Champion and move along Pets,"

Everyone hurried off.

As Jayo stared at the blue scale, a wave of unease washed over him. At last all those days and hours reading over the history books on the history and cultures of Dragnic was finally paying off. But Jayo couldn't help but feel his stomach knot at the idea of finding this dragon. He nor the history books knew if the dragons were dead. And if not, were they friendly?

CHAPTER 2

Captain Garret did what he always did on a mission, even a mission as simple as this one. He focused and analysed. If his years of service to the Emperor had taught him anything, it was the second he stop focusing. That is the second you die.

Scanning the large grey metal corridor of the Space Hulk, Garret couldn't understand nor did he care how hundreds of massive ships crashing into each other could happen. Let alone how this crashing and combining of the ships could make corridors this twisted.

Knowing his team of five heavily armed soldiers were behind him and always ready to attack, Garret focused. His large black metal gun firmly in his hand. His finger tightly on the trigger. He wasn't taking any chances.

The small curious part of him (that had been largely killed by the years of Military training) wondered how much force it could have taken to bend entire spaceships to make this corridor.

He couldn't believe how twisted and smashed up it had become. Garret smiled as he knew how interesting it would be to walk on. If not a little dangerous.

Yet the soldier part of him only cared about the mission. He never cared about his own safety. His life wasn't worth much. Garret only wanted to protect his team and serve his Emperor.

As he smelt the foul, stale air of the space hulk, Garret walked forward slowly. Holding his gun out in front of him. Despite how normal this all was for a space hulk mission, he still wanted to be careful.

Garret wore his normal black body armour with thick layers of armour plating embedded into it. His long brown hair was twisted into his normal bun. He hated how his old squad mates would mock him for his hair but he liked it.

Through his armoured booted feet, Garret felt the space hulk hum and vibrate as its coldness seemed into his boots. The last thing he wanted was to be trapped on here. He would probably freeze to death.

Hearing the space hulk creak and bang for some reason, Garret grinned as he heard his black armoured friends slowly walk behind him. They would protect him no matter what, and Garret would protect them.

Walking through the corridor, Garret was surprised how easy it was to walk through despite it looking so twisted and small back there.

As they neared the end of the corridor, Garret stopped as he heard a noisy buzzing sound. He smiled as he walked forward turning left.

He stopped as him and his team got to the broken door frame of a new room. Garret lowered his gun slightly as he realised this was what his mission was all about. The entire reason he had spent hours crawling through the space hulk all to get to this room where strange signals were apparently coming from.

Feeling the body warmth of his friends close to him, Garret focused on the room ahead. He was a bit surprised at how small it was and how perfect it was considering all the rooms, corridors and everything he had seen had been smashed to various degrees.

The small blue metal box room felt freezing as Garret and his friends stepped inside. Garret frowned at the rough, bumpy texture of the walls and floor. But what really caught their attention was the thin shiny blue metal pillar in the centre. There was something on top.

Garret crouched a little so he was eye level with the strange black flashing cube floating on top of the pillar. Garret's eyes narrowed on the circular orbs that looked embedded into the centre of each face of the cube.

This was strange.

Garret had never seen such a strange object in the middle of a space hulk. This was not a normal part of the mission. The strangest thing Garret had seen on a hulk before now was a sort of cheese like alien race that infested the hulk.

A short fully armoured man walked up to Garret carrying a flame thrower the size of a child.

"What we want to do boss?" the short man asked.

Garret didn't say anything.

Another tall muscular (and quite honestly hot) man walked over.

"Come on, Garret. Just blow it open. We need to complete the mission,"

Garret frowned. He was all for destroying things in the name of his mission and the Emperor. But he didn't want to destroy this cube. It felt important, he just didn't know why.

Focusing on the cube, Garret tried to see if there were any gaps in the cube. Maybe he could stick a knife in it and break it open and help it open.

There wasn't.

"Come on, Boss. You know we're right. Blow it!"

Garret turned and frowned. "We are not destroying this cube,"

The men muttered something and walked away.

Looking back at the cube, Garret could have sworn he saw the cube flash bright and give off a warm aura just for him. Maybe a thank you. Maybe nothing.

Garret wondered whether or not one of the scientists, professors or whatever they were on the planet below could help him open it. He shook his head at that. The last thing he wanted to do was hang round a bunch of brain boxes for any longer than necessary.

They reminded him too much of the so-called war heroes that would come home, shout out their stories and only talk when a real situation arose. These people never acted and academics were the same. Always talk. Never any action.

A green light flashed on a sleeve of his armour. He pressed it. The voice of the Master of his ship filled the little box room.

"Captain Garret, return to the ship immediately. Activate your teleporters. We can use them to get you out,"

Garret pressed another button. His armour hummed as the teleporter was activated.

Everyone else did the same.

"Done, what's happening Sir?" Garret asked.

"It's the archaeological team. They're in trouble,"

Garret rolled his eyes. He was right. These people were only good at digging and talk. But he had to serve his Emperor and right now, that meant saving the team.

CHAPTER 3

Professor Jayo couldn't contain his excitement as he watched the dig unfold. This was going to be amazing. A historical first. His stomach was filled with butterflies.

Standing on the rough crumby orange sandstone, Jayo gave a massive smile as he watched the rest of his team scrape and brush away the sandstone. He was impressed at how quickly they had worked at moving away the sandstone and finding more of the bright glowing blue scales.

Focusing on the amazing glowing scales, Jayo must have counted at least two hundred of them as they team continued to dig. The dragon creature was stunning as Jayo's eyes focused on it.

He was stunned by the size of it but he was proud of his team for digging out a full leg of the dragon. Jayo had taken some measurements earlier and he still wanted to laugh about the dragon's leg being a full three metres long.

Breathing in the cool damp air that smelt of burnt ozone, Jayo couldn't take his eyes off it. The leg was wonderous with the hundreds of glowing blue metallic scales wrapped around it.

Jayo tried to wonder how big it was going to be when it was fully uncovered. Let alone what he was going to do first. Take measurements? Scan it? He didn't know.

Feeling his eyes were starting to strain by staring the glowing scales for so long, Jayo sadly looked away and admired the massive flat open plane of sandstone around them with the massive mountain range in the distance.

He loved this planet.

Listening to the team brush and scrape away the sandstone, Jayo's feeling of butterflies returned. Yet he still didn't know too much about the dragons.

He tried to remember what the history books had said about them and sadly there wasn't much. Jayo knew the dragon creatures had their own small Empire about three hundred thousand years ago but for some reason all trace of them stopped after that.

Jayo smiled as he remembered the tens of planets and teams he had led trying to find remains of the creatures on other worlds. They all failed and Jayo frowned as he remembered how… tenuous his job had become.

Looking back at the blue scaly leg, Jayo nodded as he tried to imagine the look on the faces of his university when he came back to them with the dragon. They wouldn't be judging him then.

"Wanna a cuppa, Pet?" Saraho asked, passing Jayo a warm red mug of red coloured tea.

Nodding his thanks, Jayo took a sip and his mouth was instantly filled with the amazing tastes of strawberries and sweet oranges. It was the best drink he had had for ages.

"Thank you. How's your coffee?" Jayo asked.

"It's Champion, Pet. Wonderful,"

Jayo took another delicious sip and they both looked at the dig.

"Are you not digging Pet?"

Jayo shook his head as he tried to decide. He still had his grey metal trowel hanging from his waist. He really wanted to go down and dig but he couldn't take all the glory of the find.

"No, best let the younger ones have some fun,"

"Champion idea. What the books say about activating tha dragon?"

Jayo almost choked on his drink. "Come on girl. We can't activate it. The books say their weapons of mass destruction,"

Saraho looked up at the sky. "Pet, do ya really think the milly escort doesn't know that?"

Jayo opened his mouth but closed it. Did she have a point? Jayo remembered how the history books from various cultures had described the dragons as destroyer of worlds. He couldn't, he wouldn't let that happen to his Human Empire.

He moved closer to Saraho. "Tell you a secret.

The history books say there's a secret control temple on the planet. The dragons can only be activated from there,"

Saraho nodded. "Pet, if the dragons need to be activated. Who da activating?"

Again, Jayo opened his mouth and closed it. He knew there was a reason he kept her around!

"I don't know. The history books never said anything. I only use the term activate because it seems their machines,"

Saraho nodded and finished off her coffee.

Hearing a loud hum and bang, Jayo and Saraho walked over to the dig team. Feeling the rough crumbly sandstone under their feet as they stood next to the team. Breathing in their sweaty odours.

"Professor, it's... it's the dragon. It made a bang," someone said.

Professor Jayo knelt down and placed his palm on the dragon legs. The scales felt smooth and cold and... something jabbed him.

Jayo shot back.

He looked at his hand.

He could see something blue climbing up his arm.

Jayo panicked.

The blue thing disappeared.

The dragon creeped.

It banged.

The sandstone crumbled.

Everyone ran back.

The dragon leg twitched.
Jayo ran back to join the team.
He pressed a distress button.
Something exploded up.
Sandstone crumbled.
Sandstone was obliterated.
Sandy dust rained down.
The team screamed.
Scratching their eyes.
Their eyes burned.
Jayo wiped his eyes.
He was okay.
Saraho splashed water on her face.
She was okay.
Jayo looked at the sandstone dig.
He screamed.
Terror gripped him.
A massive blue dragon stood there.
Its metallic head roaring.
Breathing blue fire.
It looked at the team.
It looked at Jayo.
The dragon bowed its head.
Two women rushed over.
Holding guns.
Jayo tried to stop them.
The women fired.
They hit the dragon.
The dragon screamed.
It attacked.

Breathing fire.
Jayo tackled Saraho.
The fire missed them.
Their team screamed.
The flames licked their flesh.
Jayo jumped up.
He pressed the distress button again.
Saraho grabbed him.
They ran.
Jayo didn't want to leave.
He looked at his team.
The dragon chomped on them.
Slaughtering them.
Their bones crunching.
Their muscles snapping.
Their skulls shattering.
Jayo and Saraho kept running.
They had to live.
They had to warn the others.

CHAPTER 4

Captain Garret took a deep damp breath as he gripped the handrails on the top of the grey metal gunship.

As Garret felt the gunship bank and turn, he imagined the perfectly smooth aerodynamic ship slice through Dragnic's sand filled atmosphere.

Garret looked through his helmet at his friends and brothers in arms as they hung onto the handrails as the gunship continued to turn.

He had to admit he wasn't impressed that he had to go out and leave his mission just to save some Professors. But Garret knew his Emperor would want him to, so Garret felt forced to intervene.

The only piece of comfort he found was unlike other Captains and squads on the ship, Garret hadn't flat out refused to go and save the team.

He didn't know why but that disgusted him. Garret just couldn't understand why these soldiers took had taken the oath to always protect all of the

Emperor's subjects were refusing to. They were a disgrace.

Focusing on the gunship, Garret looked at each of his friends. They didn't look at him. They didn't even speak to him. Garret frowned inside his helmet, could they really be that annoyed at him for not blowing up that cube?

A small part of Garret would understand their annoyance because they were there to do a mission. The mission is the priority and soldiers must do everything they can to complete the mission.

But Garret wasn't going to destroy a cube, a piece of technology for the sake of it. Even now he couldn't explain it but he felt as if the cube was special. Maybe even alive.

Forcing those ridiculous thoughts away, Garret guessed, from the way his *friends* were preparing their weapons, that they were approaching the team of Professors.

Pressing a button on his fully armoured body, Garret made small gaps in the gunship's doors open.

Garret smiled as he saw miles upon miles of bright orange sandstone with a large mountain range in the far distance. He liked the look of it, but it was terrible. There was no way this would be a good battlefield or warzone. It's way too open.

Out of the corner of his eye, Garret saw two little dots running away from something. Garret rolled his eyes at the cowardice of these professors.

They must have heard about the horrors of the

galaxy and they must have heard about even more in their precious history books. They should be able to deal with the reality of the Empire.

Then the gunship turned a little to reveal what the Professors were running from. Garret wasn't scared, he was excited as he saw the immense dragon-like creature with its bright blue glowing scales. Its wings were the size of a football pitch and its dragon head roared.

It was amazing. Garret looked forward to shooting it.

"Squad. Land the ship. Provide cover fire. I'll get the Professors. Then we GO!" Garret said.

The others nodded but Garret knew they didn't care.

Feeling the gunship fly over to the Professors and lower, Garret held his large black metal gun and took a deep breath.

The door opened.

Garret stormed out.

His feet crumbled the sandstone.

He flew over to the professors.

He pointed to the gunship.

The dragon roared.

Garret raised his gun.

The dragon stormed over.

Garret fired.

The dragon screamed.

Chunks of metal scales flew off.

Garret laughed.

He charged over to the gunship.
His team jumped out.
They charged at the dragon.
Garret rolled his eyes.
He yelled at them.
The dragon smiled.
Whacking them with its tail.
Flapping its wing.
The gunship's engines roared.
Smoke poured out the engines.
Garret's friends fired.
The dragon roared.
Breathing fire.
Obliterating his friends.
Garret started running.
The professors grabbed him.
Garret struggled.
The dragon roared.
Garret went limp.
The Professors got him in the gunship.
They flew away.
Hearing the Dragon scream in rage behind them.

CHAPTER 5

Professor Jayo sat with his face in his hands as he sat on a cold metal box in the hangar of the *Emperor's Fist*. Jayo couldn't believe what just happened. His entire team save Saraho gone in a few minutes.

Wiping his eyes, Jayo stretched his back and tried to look around but he really didn't want to move. He didn't want to do anything. Especially, as he remembered watching his friends being burnt alive.

Trying to move those thoughts to the back of his mind, Jayo studied the massive shiny silver walls of the hangar with hundreds of bird-like fighters hanging on the walls. There must have been thousands of them just waiting to be unleashed on the enemy.

Jayo felt a bit unease in the deadly silence of the hangar. He knew the hangar was like the beating heart of the defence of a ship and he would have thought the hangar would be packed full of soldiers after what happened.

Yet he was glad it wasn't. Jayo really just wanted

to be left alone in the silence as he wondered what to do next. There were so many bodies and he was glad Saraho had wanted to sleep after what happened.

Jayo couldn't blame her. He wanted sleep more than anything but whenever he closed his eyes. All he could see were the burning bodies of his friends.

Breathing in the cool air with a hint of chlorine (Jayo knew the enviro-systems were going bad), he tried to cheer himself up by remembering the history of Empire hangars.

He laughed to himself as he realised their history was actually very diverse from the small chunky, ugly hangars of the early Empires ships to these such sleeker and perfect hangars.

Running his fingers over the smooth cold metal of the box he sat on, Jayo got out his grey metal trowel and just held it. Jayo didn't know if it would help but he always loved the feeling of it. The feeling of about to discover something amazing and hopefully career or life changing.

He turned slightly as Jayo heard someone walk towards him and at first Jayo looked back at his trowel. Then he realised it was the soldier who rescued him and Saraho.

Looking back at him, Jayo smiled and wow... this was the first time he had actually looked at the soldier and he was... hot.

Jayo couldn't help but look at his amazing smooth beautiful face with those gorgeous deep blue eyes. Jayo particularly smiled at the wonderful bun of brown hair the soldier had. He was so beautiful. And his body hiding behind his tight black t-shirt was pretty amazing too.

The soldier smiled back and pulled another metal box over and he sat opposite Jayo.

"Thank you, Professor..." the soldier said.

"Professor Jayo of the University of Jupiter, and you?"

The soldier's eyes widened at the name of the university.

"Impressive, Jayo. I'm Captain Garret of...a dead squad,"

Jayo felt bad as he saw the very hot Garret's eyes fall to the floor.

"I'm sorry for your loss. Is there anything I can do for you?" Jayo asked.

Garret looked up and his eyebrows rose.

"Shouldn't I be the one asking you that? You're the one that lost your team,"

Jayo frowned as the memories of the burning bodies returned to his mind. He didn't need the reminder. The Professor reached into a pocket and pulled out a small gold ring.

"What's that?" Garret asked.

Jayo smiled. "It was my wedding ring. My husband... he died a few years ago. He got shot by a traitor on a warzone,"

Garret leant a little closer and rubbed Jayo's hand. Jayo smiled. Pure electricity flowed between them. Jayo loved it.

Jayo tried not to frown as Garret took his hand away.

"I'm sorry to hear that. I know how it feels. I hate the traitors too. Too many friends have died by their hands,"

Jayo nodded at that. He hated these people who had betrayed the Emperor and now fought to controls the Empire for themselves. They were monsters. Jayo had seen their work too many times. So much torture and death.

Knowing he was being bold (something he had never been before), Jayo asked:

"Your wife or girlfriend must miss you?"

Garret laughed at that bad attempt to hide his interest.

"No, I don't have a girlfriend or wife. I'm more interested in our kind,"

Jayo gave Garrett an okay-I-don't-care smile and shrug. Garret shook his head.

Staring back at the beautiful Garret, a part of Jayo wanted nothing more than to hug him and undo his hairband and see how long his beautiful hair was. Despite him knowing he was just sad over his friends, Jayo still really wanted to do it.

Garret smiled at him. Jayo wasn't sure how to take it. He hadn't met another hot guy since his husband was killed.

"What's your Master of the Ship doing?" Jayo asked.

Garret frowned briefly and leant back. Jayo

wanted to kick himself as he ruined the moment.

"That's the reason why I'm here. The Master wants you up in the bridge. He wants answers and he's not happy in the slightest,"

Jayo rolled his eyes. The last thing he needed was some jump up military brat who thought himself god shouting at him.

"Will you be there?" Jayo asked, making him sound more desperate than he wanted to.

"Yes and so will your friend,"

Jayo had to stop himself from laughing at the idea of Saraho at a formal military briefing. She couldn't be formal to save her life.

Knowing this was going to be fun, Jayo stood up and Garret led them towards the bridge.

Jayo felt his grey metal trowel in his hand as he walked. He gave Garret a massive grin as he knew he was right. He always discovered something life changing (and beautiful) when he held his trowel.

CHAPTER 6

Captain Garret led Jayo into the massive Amphitheatre-like bridge of the Emperor's Fist. He was always a bit starstruck and amazed whenever he walked in here.

Garret loved it how each level of the bridge got higher and higher and filled with more and more officers looking at holographic screens.

Looking dead ahead past the ground of military people in the middle, Garret gave a small smile as he stared out through the thick glass window that went floor to ceiling, at the planet below.

Garret didn't want to hide how amazing the bright orange sandy planet of Dragnic looked from orbit. But if the past had taught him such it was that the military does not appreciate his admiration of planets. Garret knew that was probably one of his problems with the military.

Garret frowned as he smelt hints of sweet bitter oranges in the air as he pressed his back against the cold metal walls of the amphitheatre and watched the Professor walk towards the centre.

Garret felt awful for watching the Professor as he walked but he was attractive. He was hot. Just looking at *Jayo* (a very beautiful name) Garret could feel himself go lightheaded and a drip of sweat ran down his back.

A part of Garret wanted, needed to kick himself for thinking like that. He was a servant of the Emperor and his Lord and Master had sent him to Dragnic to do a mission. Not thinking about a slim Professor, who had lost his husband.

But as Garret looked at the stunning Jayo holding his grey metal trowel, he couldn't help himself but stare. Jayo was beautiful. Especially, in those baggy black trousers and loose slim-fitting black t-shirt.

The sound of swiping and talking above him reminded Garret that he was on the bridge and there were a lot of people here. He couldn't be caught staring at Jayo. Most of the soldiers didn't like him enough as it was, Garret couldn't afford them to hate him even more.

Ignoring the other soldiers that lined the wall of the amphitheatre bridge, Garret focused on the military people near Jayo. There were only three officers.

Garret's eyes narrowed as he forgot about the two guards in the centre and focused on the Master of the *Emperor's Fist*.

In all honesty, Garret never liked him and even

more Garret felt his blood boil slightly at the sight of him. He was so arrogant and demanding, not what a Master should be.

The Master of the Ship wore disgusting, posh long light blue robes with golden crescent moons sowed into the fabric. Garret wanted to look away as he looked at the Master's long Gaul face that looked unnatural and pale.

Hearing someone else enter the bridge, Garret tried not to laugh as he saw Saraho walk into the bridge like it was her own home. This was going to be interesting. But he just hoped Jayo would be okay.

"Thank you for finally joining us. You professors do take your time," the Master said, his voice rough and unloved.

"That's okay, Pet," Saraho said, looking at the Master.

The Master's frown deepened.

"Why have you summoned us here?" Jayo said in his beautiful, smooth voice.

The Master's hands formed fists. Garret prepared himself. The Master relaxed.

"Because of *your* stupid dig, my men are dead. Captain Garret is a failure. The planet is a problem now,"

Garret wanted to step forward and protest at his so-called failure but he stopped when he saw Jayo frowning at the Master. His eyes angry.

A part of Garret was shocked. He had never had someone want or look like they wanted to stand up for him before. Especially not a non-military person. Garret couldn't tell if Jayo was stupid or brave.

"What problem have *we* created?" Jayo asked.

The Master's eyes narrowed. "*You* have created the problem here, Professor,"

"I asked for a military escort. *You* denied it," Jayo said.

"I am in charge. I-"

"Master I am Professor Jayo. I have the Emperor's personal thanks. Who do you think outranks who in His eyes?"

Garret couldn't help but smile.

The Master took a long deep breath.

"You will fix this," the Master said.

He whipped out a gun.

Pointing it at Saraho.

"Or I will kill her,"

Jayo frowned.

Garret stepped forward. "Stand down, Master. He is not your enemy. Tell us what is happening,"

Everyone on the bridge stopped and looked at Garret. He wondered if any of them had made a bet on whether the Master hits him or not.

The Master eyed Garret and lowered his gun.

"Thank you, Pet,"

Garret nodded.

The Master waved his hand making the glass window of the planet below become covered in bright red holograms of dragons.

Garret tried to study them but there wasn't a

pattern. It looked so random and chaotic, there were dragons all over the planet. In the cool south, the freezing north and the boiling central regions.

A sense of adventure and wanting to kill filled Garret. He wanted to complete his mission and attack these creatures for his Emperor. He didn't want anyone else on the *Emperor's Fist* to die. Especially not Jayo.

"Ever since your mistake and your stupid dig, dragons have been awakening all over the planet. At different times. Different locations. Different sizes of Dragons,"

Garret's eyes narrowed as he saw Jayo ignore the Master and walk towards the holograms on the planet.

Garret walked forward. "See something Professor,"

"Don't be stupid, Garret. Of course he doesn't. He's a silly little-"

Garret shot a warning look at the Master.

"Saraho," Jayo said.

"Yes Pet,"

"What if these different types aren't dragons?"

Saraho smiled and walked over to Jayo. Garret did the same. He had no idea what the Professor was talking about.

"Pet what if these different types are subspecies?"

"Oh that would be amazing,"

The Master stomped on the cold grey metal

ground.

"What is your plan for stopping and killing them?"

Jayo frowned as he continued to look at the holograms.

"I am a Professor, not a killer,"

The Master walked over to Jayo.

Whipped out his gun.

Pressed it against his head.

Garret shot forward.

Soldiers grabbed him.

They whacked him in the stomach.

Garret stopped struggling.

"Professor, you might not be a killer. But I am. I will protect this ship and my people. Your lives don't matter to me,"

Saraho shook her head. "Well Pet. That's not very Champion, is it?"

"No," Jayo said.

Knowing sooner or later the Master would shoot, Garret knew he needed to speak but he had no idea what to do. He clearly didn't understand what the professors were looking at.

"*Jayo*, what do you need?" Garret asked.

For some silly reason, Garret really wanted Jayo to say he needed him, but he knew he was being silly. The Master would probably shoot them all for saying that.

Jayo continued to stare at the hologram and whisper something to Saraho. Garret tried to struggle against the soldiers but they wouldn't let him go.

"Master Pet, looky here at tha biggy hologram,"

The Master frowned and both him and Garret looked at the largest red hologram in the far north of the planet.

"What!" the Master shouted.

Jayo waved his fingers in the air. "I believe this is an ancient temple construct. The history books are filled with references to these places,"

The Master nodded.

"Tha books say the large amount of dragons are always found neat tha temples, Pet,"

The Master smiled and Garret was concerned he might crack his own face. The Master turned to Garret.

"You alone with go with them,"

Garret was about to protest.

"Captain Garret, you are a failure. You allowed your team to die. You should have died with them. Go with the Professors or I will make you join your team. The choice is yours,"

Looking at Jayo, Garret didn't want to go with them. He didn't want to be responsible for Jayo's safety but Garret didn't know if he would trust anyone else with this beautiful man's safety.

Nodding to the Master, Garret turned around and left with the beautiful Jayo and Saraho behind him. Garret just wanted to complete his mission and keep Jayo safe.

CHAPTER 7

Professor Jayo stepped out of the perfectly aerodynamic silver gunship and immediately felt the bitter cold of the far north of Dragnic. He hated the cold, he hadn't even expected it to be this cold.

But what amazed him even more was despite the freezing air, that made him shiver, the massive dragon temple was in the centre of another immense plane of orange sandstone.

Jayo cocked his head as he looked at the ground. There was something strange about the sandstone. He remembered when he first got to the planet he thought it was strange how the planet was made completely from sandstone. Jayo still didn't know how it happened. It shouldn't be possible, but it was.

Breathing in the freezing cold air that felt like it coated his lungs in ice with every breath, Jayo stared up at the massive orange sandstone cone in front of them.

Jayo shook his head as he realised that this was

the amazing dragon temple he had wanted to find. He hadn't expected it to look like this at all. After all, this was only a massive cone that was made of pure sandstone. It wasn't grand but it wasn't small.

Jayo's eyes narrowed on the cone itself and he noticed Saraho was doing the same. They both knew the cone was a little off, it was too perfect for a planet like Dragnic. Through the geological processes alone the cone would have been damaged and chipped.

But it was a perfectly smooth cone. Too smooth to be natural.

Hearing the clicking and humming of gorgeous Garret's gun, Jayo tried not to smile too much as he turned to face that beautiful soldier.

Jayo wanted to try and impress Garret with his knowledge (or lack thereof) of the history of these dragon temples. But instead he could only stare at Garret and admire his well-fitting body armour, his smooth wonderful face and that beautiful bun of long brown hair.

If Jayo was at university, he probably would have kicked himself for thinking like this, he was a serious academic. (Well he used to be before people started hating him) Jayo didn't stare and get lost in people's amazing looks. He didn't know why or what was so different with Garret?

Seeing Garret smile back at him, Jayo felt his heart thump and he turned back to the dragon temple. And he smiled as he saw a little imperfection in the cone.

Pointing at it, Saraho nodded and they all walked towards what looked like a little gap in-between the edges of the cone.

After a few minutes, Jayo led the team to the gap, and he instantly remembered what it felt like to be at the bottom of a canyon and look up. Seeing stone rise high, high above you.

Jayo cocked his head as he wondered how it was formed and the purpose of it. His mind started to think about the weather processes, the history of the dragon and so much more.

A dragon roar ripped through the air.

Jayo walked into the small sandstone gap between the edges of the canyon. The others followed him and Jayo was surprised the gap was so small considering dragons use to use this temple. Or did they?

Jayo wanted to find out.

After a few minutes of walking through the small sandstone gap, Jayo's mouth dropped as they entered an amazing inner chamber inside the temple. Jayo couldn't believe how amazing it looked.

Taking a deep breath and forcing his mind to stop, there was a large plain looking dome in the middle. But Jayo was instantly excited as he saw all the little details of the perfectly smooth domed chamber of the temple. It was amazing. Jayo couldn't even start to understand how the dragons had got this immense chamber so smooth without machines.

Jayo's eyes widened as he considered the

possibility of the dragons having machines. They were metal and machines, so could they have machines? That could rewrite the history books if the dragons were more advance than previously thought.

Really forcing himself to stop thinking so much, Jayo focused on the various dragon heads high up on the domed ceiling. They were large and very close to the top of the cone. Jayo wasn't sure their purpose but they were probably just decorative.

Walking into the inner chamber some more, Jayo smiled when he heard Saraho give a massive gasp of amazement and she started to walk around quickly. He wouldn't want to be inside her mind. His was busy enough.

Breathing in the dusty, stale air of the chamber, Jayo fought the urge to gag as the chamber was disturbed for probably the first time in millions of years.

The sound of howling wind outside made Jayo frowned as he wondered what was the chance of a sandstorm so far north. He hoped that wouldn't be the case.

"Pet, Laddie look at this," Saraho said.

Garret ignored her and kept looking around.

Jayo cocked his head and his eyes narrowed as he looked at the centre of the chamber. At first he had dismissed it because it looked like a plain sandstone dome in the middle that was waist high. But as Jayo focused on it, it looked more interesting.

Walking over to Saraho, Jayo's eyebrows rose as

he saw Saraho point towards a little dragon symbol that looked to be eating a snake.

Both Saraho and Jayo looked at each other. He remembered all the ecological scans he did when they first arrived. There were no snakes on the planet, so why draw one here?

Jayo crouched a little bit so he was eye level with the symbol. He couldn't understand why they'd put a symbol on a sandstone dome. What if it wasn't a plain dome?

Getting out his trusty grey metal trowel, Jayo smiled as he tapped the dome gently. Sandstone crumbled away revealing something glowing blue behind it.

Saraho crouched down next to him. Jayo held out his palm and he felt like he was being scanned.

Moments later, the sandstone crumbled away. Revealing a large metal dome glowing dark blue that was humming to life.

Standing up Jayo smiled as his gorgeous Garret wandered over clearly impressed and Saraho hugged him.

A bright blue hologram of the planet flared to life. Including the *Emperor's Fist* and the space hulk in orbit with lots of bright green spots on the planet.

"What's that *Jayo*?" Garret asked.

Jayo loved the way garret said his name.

"I don't know. It looks like the map is showing us a live feed of the planet. I think the dragons were more advance than we knew,"

"I agree Pet. Tha books always said dragons were just that dragons. They never said techie,"

"Probably because we never found any technology. We haven't on our digs," Jayo said.

Garret pointed to the glowing yellow dot in the north.

"Is that us?"

Jayo nodded. "Probably but…"

He couldn't help but feel the map was off slightly and very wrong. It couldn't be a fault because the map showed the *Emperor's Fist* in perfect position.

Saraho started nodding. "Oh Pet, that's Champion. Very clever of ya dragons,"

Garret shook his head. "Someone care to explain,"

Jayo pointed to the glowing yellow dot and Saraho showed Garret a true map of the planet using his army-issued dataslate.

"You see Garret, everything on the planet is off by a factor of three thousand. On the hologram it looks tiny but in real life it's massive,"

Garret slowly nodded. "Why do it?"

The howling wind outside got louder.

"Pet, if ya hiding something. How best to keep ya enemy away?"

Garret walked over to Jayo. Jayo loved the feeling of Garret's warm body so close to him.

"Where are we heading next?" Garret asked.

The non-academic part of him so badly wanted to suggest something… biological but Jayo was too focused on the academics here. This temple chamber alone was enough to rewrite history.

A loud roar ripped through the chamber.

The ground shook.

A dragon head smashed onto the ground.

CHAPTER 8

Captain Garret felt the massive orange sandstone dome shake and vibrate. His military training kicked in. He guessed he might only have a minute or two before the dragons attacked.

He needed to think.

Looking around Garret clocked the massive sandstone dragon heads were shaking. They were bound to fall off any moment. There was no escape up.

Breathing in the sandy damp cool air of the dome, Garret turned to face the small gap they had entered the dome through. It was shaking. Garret had no idea how much longer the gap would last until it collapsed.

As much as he hated it for being like a canyon that could collapse on top of them at any moment.

It was their only escape.

Hearing another dragon roar rip through the air, Garret pressed his fingers hard against the cold black metal of his gun. He was going to be prepared.

Turning to the two Professors, Garret wanted to stare and admire his beautiful Jayo with that amazing face and hair. But he had to protect Jayo and Saraho.

Garret frowned at the professors. They were both too busy studying the massive holographic map of the planet in the middle of the chamber.

The sandstone dome temple shook.

Sandstone dragon heads smashed.

Kicking up dust.

The air was thick with dust.

Garret cleared his eyes.

The Professors screamed.

The temple exploded.

A dragon tailed smashed into the temple.

Obliterating the top of the temple.

Sandstone crashed around them.

The hologram was annihilated.

Garret charged over.

He grabbed the Professors.

Dragging them to the sandstone gap.

He pushed them through.

More sandstone smashed around him.

The Professors ran through the gap.

Garret was about to join them.

A massive metallic claw stomped behind it.

Garret spun.

It was a massive dragon.

It roared.

Garret fired.

He charged.

Running through the gap.

He charged out of it.

His feet destroying the sandstone ground.

He kept running.

Garret could see the aerodynamic grey gunship.

It was taking off.

The Professors were flying in.

Garret hurried.

He flew at it.

Another dragon roar ripped through the air.

The gunship was about to leave.

Garret jumped.

He was about to miss.

He slashed at the air.

His fingers missed the gunship.

He was falling.

Saraho grabbed his arm.

Pulling him in.

Jayo punched the controls.

The gunship flew off.

Feeling the cold metal deck as he fell on it, Garret took long deep breaths as he tried to recover from his extreme run. He loved the action and a good run but that was a little extreme even for him.

Not bothering to move, Garret simply laid there catching his breath. He could still smelt the damp sand air with new hints of sweat from his running. Garret still wouldn't have it any other way.

Hearing the engines hum and spatter a little,

Garret rolled his eyes as he wondered if some sand or worse had gotten into the engines. Maybe he could check it out later, but for now all he wanted to do was lay here and recover.

He still couldn't believe the power of that dragon. Garret had barely seen it probably because the attack had happened so fast. But it still unnerved him.

When a beautiful man stood over him wearing his amazing loose black t-shirt and those wonderful baggy trousers, Garret couldn't help but smile as he looked at Jayo.

If he was a teenager, Garret had no doubt he would kick Jayo to the floor to join him. He was surprised it was so relaxing laying down on the cold metal deck of the gunship.

"You okay?" Jayo asked.

Garret simply nodded. He wasn't going to show any weakness in front of his beautiful Jayo.

Jayo sat down next to Garret and he placed Garret's hand in his. Garret wasn't going to say no.

"Thanks for getting us out. I plotted our coordinates to our next stop,"

"Where's that?" Garrett asked.

"Me and Saraho managed to find the correct location of another much larger temple. Maybe that can give us some answers,"

Garret smiled and rubbed Jayo's smooth soft hands.

"You're very clever,"

"I try,"

"So do I Pet," Saraho said, walking over with a puzzled look on her.

"What's wrong?" Jayo asked.

"Just ran some orbit-y scans, Pet. There are five new ships,"

Garret's eyes narrowed. He wanted to ask more but these were Professors. They weren't military soldiers who could tell one signature of a ship from another. Let alone tell by looking at the ship if it was friendly or not.

But this was weird. He hadn't heard anything about new ships joining the *Emperor's Fist*. Pushing those thoughts away, Garret shook it off as probably the Master not telling him things. The idiot.

"How long until we reach this *much larger temple?*" Garret asked.

Jayo rubbed Garret's hand. "Judging by our speed and the weather conditions-"

Three massive roars ripped through the air.

Garret tensed.

He shot up.

Something smashed into the gunship.

Ripping its back off.

Garret flew out.

Jayo grabbed him.

The gunship screamed.

Chunks of metal flew off.

They were going down.

CHAPTER 9

Professor Jayo gripped Garret's strong beautiful arms as the gunship went down.

Jayo could feel the air whip past him. The air was screaming.

Jayo wanted to try and do something but he couldn't. He could only hold on as the gunship plummeted towards the ground.

The air was screaming past him. Jayo couldn't hear anything else.

The gunship smashed into the ground.

Jayo flew out.

Landing in cold wet sandstone.

Forcing him to stand up, Jayo felt his entire body ache as it tried to deal with being thrown out of a crashing gunship. Everything from his feet to his chest to his back ached.

Looking around Jayo tried to see but his vision was cloudy. He could barely make out the massive endless orange sandstone plane they had crashed on.

It was so open.

A part of Jayo wondered if his gorgeous Garret would have preferred to crash somewhere less exposed and opened. Jayo supposed if the dragons had attacked him then this would be the perfect place to ambush them.

There was no hope for escape here.

Smelling thick black smoke and smouldering technology, Jayo's vision cleared and his mouth dropped as he saw the wreckage of the gunship engulfed in flames, pumping out massive columns of toxic black smoke.

He took a step forward.

He fell to the ground.

Feeling the orange sandstone crumble slightly under his weight, Jayo wanted to crawl over to the wreckage to make sure Saraho and Garret were okay. He knew his and Saraho's adventurous lifestyle would kill them at some point. But not today. It couldn't be today.

Jayo tried to crawl forward at the idea of his gorgeous Garret being in trouble but his body ached too much.

"What ya doing down there, Pet?" Saraho said.

Jayo shook his head and smile as he looked up at Saraho, who didn't have a single cut or burn mark on her. Maybe she would survive a little longer.

She helped Jayo up and Jayo gave a relieved moan when he saw Garret's face and wonderful brown hair in his tight bun slowly wander over to them.

Just seeing Garret was okay made Jayo relax a little. He wanted to jump on Garrett and give him a hug but Jayo didn't want him to think he was clingy or desperate. He was just glad Garret was okay.

"What was that?" Jayo asked.

Garret held his black metal gun loosely and looked around.

"Those damn dragons," he said.

Jayo wanted to say something but he felt something in his hand move and pulse warm energy up his arm. It felt nice compared to the cold air.

Three blue dragons landed around them.

They were trapped.

The dragons stomped their metallic feet.

Garret tensed.

Aiming his gun.

But Jayo didn't do anything. Watching the dragons circle the three of them, Jayo was sure there was something more to these dragons.

His eyes narrowed on the beautiful glowing blue metallic scales of each dragon. They were so beautiful and wondrous but they didn't feel dangerous.

Jayo remembered the history books spoke about the dragons as cruel, destroyer of worlds but as he looked at them and their long scaly dragon heads. Jayo didn't see monsters, he saw creatures inspecting them. Like a cat who had just discovered a new object, not quite sure of it just yet.

Garret aimed his gun.

Jayo felt his hand glow a little and he placed his hand over Garret's gun. Making him lower it.

The dragons stopped and lowered their heads a little. One dragon even lowered his massive metallic head down to Jayo's eye level. Jayo walked towards it, wondering if it was their leader.

"What are you doing!" Garret shouted.

Holding out his hand, Jayo could feel it glowing a faint blue and the dragons seemed to relax a little.

"Since I touched that dragon, I felt something inside me. I don't think these dragons want to kill us,"

"What about tha team, Pet?"

"And my friends?"

"The military team was self-defence. Our Team I'm not sure,"

The leader dragon approached Jayo slowly and it looked like it was smiling. Revealing rows upon rows of terrifying metallic teeth. Jayo tried to relax. He hoped he was right.

"Saraho, our team must have been down to faulty programming. Think about three million years asleep. There must have been… a power reboot,"

Jayo could hear Saraho whisper and explain it to Garret.

Placing his glowing hand gently on the snout of the massive blue metallic dragon, Jayo smiled as a trace of power shot up his arm.

Rubbing the dragon's snout gently, Jayo said:

"It's okay. We aren't going to hurt you. Us three will protect you,"

The dragon seemed to nod and kiss Jayo's glowing hand before flying away. Jayo needed to remember this day for the rest of his life. It was amazing.

Saraho and Garret walked over to him and they all smiled at each other. Jayo wasn't exactly sure why but it felt like they all had just witnessed something precious, that no one else in the Human Empire (save maybe the Emperor) would ever see. It was like their own personal secret.

"I sent a distress call to the Emperor's Fist. It should be a few hours before they can be bothered to answer it," Garret said, holding a military issue black dataslate.

Jayo nodded. He fully intended to use this time to get to know Garret and hopefully undo Garrett's bun, and run his fingers through his gorgeous long brown hair.

CHAPTER 10

Captain Garret stared out into the distance and looked at all the miles upon miles of flat orange sandstone as he sat.

He knew what his beautiful Jayo had done had scared off the three dragons but he still felt uneasy. He was a military man so the idea of the enemy going away and not attacking seemed... silly. But if the Professors thought the dragons were gone maybe Garret would trust them.

Feeling the soft orange sandstone crumble under his weight slightly, Garret remembered what he had thought about professors earlier. Something about academics only talk and don't do any action when it comes down to it.

Garret had to smile at that comment now. He hated how wrong he had been, these professors might have been braver than some of his old friends. The fools.

He cocked his head at that idea. What if it wasn't

Garret's fault they were dead? What if the Master of the *Emperor's Fist* was wrong?

Smelling the hints of smouldering wreckage of the gunship and the traces of black smoke in the air, Garret nodded. He was right and if what the professors had said was correct. Then he didn't need to feel guilty for watching his friends die. It was their fault for attacking the dragons instead of evacuating the professors like he ordered.

He wasn't guilty. Garret felt a massive wave of relief wash over him as he realised that.

The sound of the last remaining flames crackle on the wreckage made Garret turn slightly to see Saraho crouching near the wreckage and throwing sand at it. He didn't even want to know what she was doing. Maybe some sort of experiment.

Out of the corner of his eye, Garret saw his amazing, beautiful Jayo sat down opposite him. Garret stared briefly at his beautiful smooth face and that amazing loose black t-shirt. Jayo smiled at Garret.

Garret couldn't believe how amazing he looked even after surviving a crash and being attacked. So few soldiers even looked that good after surviving less.

Seeing Jayo was smiling and looking at the bright night sky, Garret did the same and he couldn't see what the fuss was about. Sure there were thousands of bright stars in the sky including the Emperor's Fist and those other ships. But they were just that, stars and ships.

Garret wondered for a moment what the professor saw. Maybe he saw processes happening, the travelling of light and all that stuff. Garret shook his head and focused back on the beautiful man opposite him.

"What do you see?" Garret asked.

Jayo laughed at the question. "I see the stars travelling at thousands of miles per hour. Emitting light so far away we don't even know if the star is still there. The light can still be travelling towards us but the light source would be dead,"

Garret's eyes widened.

"I see millions of solar systems. Some filled with aliens, some filled with humans, all filled with amazing opportunities for the Emperor. And some filled with… traitors,"

Garret could see Jayo's fear and sadness grip him as he said that. His shoulder rolled forward and his entire body lost its confidence.

"I'm sorry," Garret said.

"You must think me as weak or pathetic. You must have fought the traitors lots of times,"

Garret moved a little closer. "Yes, it doesn't make it any easier. Seeing those humans twisted and deranged. Saying… all sorts of hateful things towards our Emperor. Wanting the Empire to burn. It isn't easy,"

Jayo looked at the sandstone ground.

"How did it happen if you don't might me asking? Garret asked.

Jayo looked into Garret's eyes. Garret liked it.

"Me and my husband were on holiday exploring the ancient wrecks of Gallicu 9. It was amazing. Those wrecks are impressive," Jayo said, smiling.

Garret's eyebrows rose. He remembered passing them from a mission a few years ago. Jayo was right they were impressive. Garret knew it was great how the wrecks had survived for so long, but he was more impressed by the weapons on those ships.

"Then the traitors must have infiltrated the system because they took the planet so quickly. My husband Harro was a soldier so he tried to fight. He wanted to defend his Glorious Emperor's Realm,"

Garret braced for the ending.

"The traitors, their leader actually *The Herald of The End*, such a stupid name. grabbed my husband and made me stare into his eyes and he crushed his bones and crushed the life out of him,"

Garret's mouth dropped. He didn't know what to say. Garret had only heard whispers of The Herald of The End, he always believed it to be a scary story to keep recruits in line.

"I'm sorry,"

"Don't be Garret. I'm sure you've seen worse,"

Garret opened his mouth and wanted to tell him he had, but he hadn't. Garret had seen his friends die, been tortured, blown up. But never had he seen the love of his life crushed to death in front of him.

Jayo moved closer. Garret loved the feeling of his body warmth so close to him.

Seeing Jayo was staring back at the ground, Garret put his arm around Jayo's shoulder. Jayo fell into his arm and Garret couldn't, didn't want to imagine what Jayo had experienced. As a soldier, Garret knew with absolute certainty that he was meant to stare at all danger and never show fear. He believed in that tenant. He believed solely in the ability and the mission of the Emperor. But even Garret doubted he could survive what Jayo did without being harmed.

A part of Garret wanted to push Jayo away and send him on the first ship far away from Dragnic. He didn't want to let Jayo into his heart so Garret might hurt him. He couldn't do that. He wouldn't want to, but what if it happened?

Trying to get those ideas out of his mind, Garret turned his attention to those strange new ships in orbit. He had tried to scan them but nothing came up. Not a designation. Not a signature. Not a name. Nothing. They were ghosts. Garret hoped the Master of the Ship could tell him what they were when he returned.

Feeling Jayo move, Garret looked at the beautiful man and saw him stare into Garret's deep blue eye. They leant in closer. Garret loved the feeling as their lips grazed each other.

The sound of a gunship flying through the air made Garret pull away. He didn't want to, but he didn't want the soldiers on the gunship to see.

He just hoped he hadn't missed his chance with

Jayo.

CHAPTER 11

Professor Jayo felt a little disappointed about Garret moving away from the kiss as he walked into the massive amphitheatre of the bridge on board the *Emperor's Fist*.

Holding his grey metal trowel that felt cold in his fingers, Jayo's eyes narrowed as he looked around. Studying each of the metal tiers of the amphitheatre filled with rows upon rows of black armoured officers swiping and tapping at holographic computers.

As Jayo smelt the perfectly recycled air with hints of bitter sweet oranges, Jayo cocked his head at the rows of thick black armoured soldiers lining the floor of the bridge.

He remembered there were soldiers standing there before. Gorgeous Garret was one of them but they hadn't closed their helmets before. It was like looking at black armoured humanoid robots. Not very friendly!

Even the massive glass window that went floor

to ceiling on the bridge with a full view of the orange Dragnic was off slightly. Jayo remembered Garret was a bit unsure of the new ships and as Jayo looked at them he agreed.

Thinking about the ships, Jayo focused on their long sausage-like shape with thick dark blue metal plates for armour. Their bridge was near the back and looked almost like a church from ancient earth.

Using his classes and history books, Jayo smiled as he realised they were probably from three thousand years ago and made for the War of Masters in the far galactic southeast.

Then Jayo shrugged as he realised as interesting as the history was. It wasn't going to help him right now. But Jayo's eyes widened as he remembered that he recognised them. He just didn't know where from.

Hearing the swiping and buzzing of the holographic computers, Jayo turned to Saraho who was also looking about frantically. Jayo knew he wasn't wrong about the bridge. There was something wrong.

Very wrong.

As Jayo turned to gorgeous Garret with his beautiful brown bun of hair, Jayo rolled his eyes as he saw Garret's smooth face wasn't puzzled. He clearly didn't see anything was wrong.

The sound of a foot-stomping against the hard metal floor made Jayo turned and cock his head as he focused on the three figures in the middle of the bridge.

They were odd.

Jayo dismissed the tall arrogant idiot of the Master of the Ship in this typical long white robes that Jayo wanted to rip off and punch him.

Instead both Jayo and Saraho circled the two figures standing next to the Master. Jayo didn't like their long shadowy black cloaks that hid their tall (presumably) muscular bodies. Jayo didn't know if they were alien or not.

The Master stomped his foot.

Garret punched something.

Jayo spun.

Men grabbed Garret.

He struggled.

Garret was pinned.

Jayo went to help but turned to the foul Master instead. His eyes narrowed on the Master.

"Release him now!" Jayo shouted.

One of the cloaks figures clicked their fingers and the long black cloak burnt away. Revealing the most horrific person Jayo had ever met.

Jayo fell to the floor as he looked at the massive bulky blood red armour of The Herald of The End. He hadn't changed a bit since he slaughtered Jayo's husband. Jayo couldn't believe it.

The Herald's face was fallen and twisted on one side. Jayo guessed it was from an attack of some sort but the Herald looked horrific. Some many slashes and scars littered his face.

A tear started to form in Jayo's eye as he focused

on the other side of The Herald's face. Jayo recognised that smooth perfect skin and their strong cheekbones anyway.

The Herald had sown half of his husband's face onto his own.

Jayo didn't know whether to scream or not. This was an outrage and he was an abomination. How was he here? Jayo wanted to attack but he had no energy.

"Traitor!" Garret shouted, getting a punch him his stomach.

The Master laughed. "Don't be so foolish Garret. We have been serving our Lord Herald for years. Every kill, every mission has been in service to the Lord Herald," the Master said, bowing to the Herald.

Jayo saw the pain and agony in Garret's eyes. He could only imagine how much pain he must have been in. Knowing your life's work had been in service to the enemy and not the Emperor.

Saraho stood next to Jayo. "Well, this isn't very champion Flower. Isn't it?" she said to the Herald.

The Herald's twisted lips frowned.

"Why are you here?" Jayo asked fighting back his rage.

The Master was about to speak but the Herald pointed to him.

"You have served us well, mortal. You activated the dragons. On behalf of the traitors, I thank you, fool,"

Jayo's eyes widened. "This was all a plan,"

The Herald gave a twisted laugh. "Foolish

Mortal, of course it was. Did you really think a warship would accompany such a stupid little team?"

Jayo couldn't believe he had missed it. It all seemed so simple now but he had wanted to prove himself right and those people at his university wrong so bad. He wanted to be successful and acclaimed, Jayo hated this mindset before.

The Herald shook his twisted head. "Pathetic Mortal. That is why I am the superhuman and you are not,"

Jayo snarled. "A superhuman crafted by the Glorious Emperor himself. You betrayed him. And for what?"

The herald waved his hand.

Garret got kicked and punched in the stomach.

"Little mortal soldier, I served your Emperor. I thought the same as you. He was divine. Righteous. But he is all a lie. He will damn humanity in the end. So why not speed up the process?"

Saraho spat at him. "I might not be a soldier, Flower. But I know loyalty. Ya ain't loyal,"

The Herald slapped her.

Saraho smiled. "That ain't champion ya know. Tha Emperor gonna come for you,"

The Herald laughed at her. "And here I thought you were a chavy disgraceful Mortal. Turns out you're just an idiot,"

Saraho took a bow. Jayo didn't know what to do. Maybe Garett and Saraho were thinking up a plan, Jayo wanted to help but he couldn't think. Perhaps he could just buy them time.

"Why do you want to activate the Dragons?" he asked.

The Master stepped forward. "You said it yourself Professor, the history books say they're destroyer of worlds. Think of all the worlds in the Human Empire that stand against the traitors. Think how many would stand after the dragons attack?"

Jayo's eyes widened. He couldn't allow that.

"I won't help you!" Jayo shouted.

The Herald laughed so much Jayo thought he might fall over.

"I don't need you Mortal. You will help me in the end but I don't need you. I can and will kill you all. Like I did your husband,"

Jayo's eyes narrowed.

The Herald turned to face the planet below. "Take them away,"

Garret moaned and struggled.

Jayo could hear the soldiers getting closer.

"Ya ain't taking them, Flower,"

The Herald turned to her. "I am,"

"No you ain't!"

Saraho flew at the Herald.

Jayo tried to grab her.

She was too quick.

She flew at the Herald.

The Herald spun.

Grabbing her head.

Smashing it to the ground.

Her skull shattered.

Blood squirted everywhere.

Jayo sunk to his knees as he looked at the puddle of deep rich red blood that was boiling to the touch with chunks of brain and skull mixed into it.

Jayo's body went limp as he felt the soldiers grab him and pull him away.

He just kept staring at the shattered body of his best friend.

CHAPTER 12

Captain Garret felt his stomach ache from the punches that slammed into it earlier. The freezing cold metal of the grey floor in the prison cell helped but he hated all of this.

As he laid there, staring up into the bright white light of the prison cell, he couldn't think of anything else except the betrayal that was happening.

His entire life was about serving and protecting the Emperor's Realm, killing the traitors and completing his mission. But Garret knew he had failed.

He had failed himself, his beautiful Jayo but most importantly his Emperor. Garret didn't believe in the common myth that the Emperor was a divine being that guided humanity like a beacon in the darkness. But Garret hated to imagine what the Emperor would think of him at a time like this.

Casting his mind back, Garret remembered a lesson he had learnt from his training days as a soldier. It was something about pretending to serve the Emperor but serving the enemy is the great insult to His on Earth.

Feeling the freezing cold metal underneath him, Garret couldn't disagree. He felt like he had walked up to the Emperor and spat on his face.

Garret frowned as he remembered all he had wanted to do since he was a boy was serve and fight for the Emperor. He was sick of hearing his friends lose parents to the aliens and traitors. He wanted to make a difference.

As Garret breathed in the poor recycled foul air of the prison cell, he tried to think of a plan to escape but he didn't want to move. He didn't want to do anything. A small part of him just wanted to lay here and die. Maybe that was his punishment for this betrayal to the Emperor.

But was it a betrayal?

Garret cocked his head and stared hard into the bright white light in the prison cell, he actually didn't know if he was a traitor. Sure, he had aided the traitors for the past few years but it wasn't willing or knowing. He could redeem himself.

He could save the day and complete his mission.

Standing up, Garret tried to ignore the thumping pain of his stomach as he looked around the small grey metal prison cell.

He smiled as he saw a tall beautiful man laying on a small metal bench. Professor Jayo smiled back like he knew something.

Utter happiness filled Garret as he knew Jayo was okay. All he wanted to do in that moment was hug and kiss Jayo. But he knew he had to serve his Emperor and stop the traitors first.

Jayo offered Garret a smooth hand and Garret took it, helping Jayo up. He loved breathing in Jayo's sweet manly scent.

"Professor, I take it you have a plan," Garret said.

"At first I didn't. I was thinking too much about Saraho,"

"I'm sorry about her. I…"

"You should have protected her more. I'm sure you believe that but Saraho died fighting for what she believed in. She believed in the Human Empire and so do I!"

Garret smiled and nodded. He could feel his own energy starting to return. He wanted to fight these traitors head on.

Jayo made Garret focus on the bright red holographic door that Garret hadn't noticed before. It created a strange buzzing sound that Garret wasn't keen on.

"I remember reading a book on the history of prison cells,"

"Of course you did," Garret said.

"This is a Mark 5.2 Warship, correct?"

Garret paused. He tried to remember.

"Yes, I joined the crew six years ago and the ship was twenty years old then. That sounds about right,"

"Excellent!" Jayo shouted.

Garret's eyebrows rose as he leant against the freezing cold metal wall next to the holographic door.

"Why's that?" he asked.

"Well, Captain. For those in the know, there's a notorious fault for the prison cells in this model-"

Garret tensed as two black armoured guards walked past. They didn't seem to notice anything.

"What's this fault? It's impossible. We would have upgraded if there was a fault,"

"Come on, when the Navy discovered the fault. They ordered Mars to stop all productions of the Mark 5.2 and Mars agreed to hide it. Only three thousand 5.2 ships got created. To the Empire that's nothing. Leading to the Mark 6,"

Garret nodded. It sounded like something the Central Naval Command would do and… Mars was Mars. Nothing surprised Garret anymore about Mars.

"What's the fault?" Garret asked again.

"Oh yes," Jayo said, kneeling down to the bottom of the holographic door.

Garret joined him and they found a small panel. Breaking it open, Garret smiled as his fingers briefly touched Jayo's.

Jayo moved away and Garret turned his attention to the series of flashing lights under the holographic door.

"When I break this, you need to be ready," Jayo said.

Garret paused. A wave of self-doubt washed over

him. He didn't know if he could protect Jayo, Saraho had already died on his watch. He didn't want to, he couldn't lose Jayo.

He rolled his eyes as he realised how silly he was being. Garret never ever acted like this. He was a proud soldier who never hesitated to fight the enemy. But this wasn't a normal time, he wanted to protect Jayo.

Garret allowed a teenage smile to form as he finally realised that he actually did… care about Jayo. This wasn't some childish crush or some meaningless fling. He actually cared about the Professor.

Taking a deep breath, Garret prepared himself. He was ready to fight.

"Do it," Garret said.

Jayo kicked the flashing lights.

They shattered.

The door disappeared.

They charged forward.

CHAPTER 13

Professor Jayo charged out of the prison cell and felt disappointed as there were no threats nor enemies about. A small part of him wanted to be happy about that but Jayo wanted to prove to Garret that he was a fighter, and he was brave.

Focusing on the pentagonal corridor made from reinforced grey metal walls, Jayo frowned as he saw right through the silly mistakes of mark 5.2. Jayo shook his head it was no wonder why production got stopped. It wouldn't have taken much to get through these metal walls.

Jayo followed Garret as he carefully stalked the corridor, Jayo supposed he should be worried about the enemy and traitor superhumans attacking them, but he felt perfectly safe next to Garret.

Hearing the buzzing of holographic doors and the shouting of people trapped inside, Jayo cocked his head as he passed. What if these people were innocent?

He stopped outside one prison cell and stared coldly in the eyes of a squad of soldiers. They didn't look dangerous but Jayo had no idea what a dangerous person looked like. For all Jayo knew these were traitors or serial killers.

The smell of burnt ozone and seared flesh, oddly enough, reminded Jayo of his mother's roast dinner from a few decades ago. Jayo shook his head at how weird his memory was.

Staring straight ahead, Jayo tried not to give gorgeous Garret a boyish grin as Jayo watched him move, and his brown hair bun moved a little. He was so beautiful.

Continuing to walk through the corridor, Jayo remembered the traitors had let him keep his grey metal trowel. Jayo took it out and held it out in front of him. He had no idea if it was a good weapon. He had never had a reason to try it.

Garret stopped ahead. Jayo looked around him to see a harmless section of the corridor where it ran into another one. Jayo looked at a small back cupboard without a door to one side.

Garret pushed him inside.

Jayo hated himself but he got excited by it. Garret placed his strong rough hand over Jayo's mouth. He didn't know whether or not to be excited now.

Moments later two superhuman traitors walked past in their disgusting black armour. Jayo was still shocked by the size of them, they must have been three times the height of a normal human.

Garret took his hand away and placed it over his lips looking at Jayo. Jayo nodded. Watching Garret slide out of the cupboard, Jayo took a step forward to watch.

His eyes widened as he saw Garret sneak forward and snap the necks of the superhumans.

Their corpses fell to the ground. Garret grabbed their guns and walked back up. He threw Jayo a gun.

He took it and they kept walking but the heavy metal grey gun felt strange to Jayo. Jayo knew exactly how to fire one but he still wasn't sure that he wanted to use it.

The memories of his husband fighting and being slaughtered filled his mind. Ever since that moment, Jayo had hated violence and guns yet he knew guns were needed for protection in this case.

A small part of him wanted to ask Garret to take it for him. But Jayo rolled his eyes as he knew that would have made him look weak and just another pathetic academic that couldn't defend themselves.

Jayo took a deep breath as he remembered Saraho's skull shattering. At the time it didn't seem natural or like it was real.

Knowing he couldn't afford to break, not on an enemy ship filled with traitors, Jayo took a deep breath and focused on looking out for traitors. He had to try and protect Garret after all. Jayo didn't want to lose him.

The two men turned another corner into a large

pentagonal corridor that was near the hangar.

Shots fired.

Bullets screamed through the air.

Garret grabbed Jayo.

Pulling him back round the corner.

Garret fired.

Jayo poked his head round.

Three traitors.

Normal humans.

Jayo whipped his head back round the corner.

Garret fired.

Someone screamed.

More bullets slammed into the metal.

They didn't have much time.

Jayo aimed.

Jayo went to fire.

He didn't want to.

Garret hissed.

He was in danger.

Jayo fired.

Someone's chest exploded.

Garret fired.

The last one exploded.

Garret grabbed Jayo.

Pulling him along.

More screams came from behind.

They ran.

Jayo ran as fast as he could.

Bullets screamed towards them.

Smashing into the wall.

Jayo kept running.
Lights exploded ahead.
Jayo couldn't see.
He didn't know where he was going.
Garret grabbed him.
Pulling and pushing him.
Jayo smiled.
Garret must know the route.
Heat shot past him.
The bullets were getting closer.
Jayo turned another corner.
Then another.
Then another.
Bright flames lit up the corridor.
Garret kept running.
Jayo did the same.
Flames chased them.
Jayo hated flamethrowers.
Jayo saw light ahead.
He heard Garret reload his gun.
Garret aimed.
Jayo was confused.
There was nothing to aim at.
They kept running.
A metal door opened.
Bullets flew everywhere.
Jayo blinked.
They were in the hangar.
He knew where to go.
Jayo charged.

He wasn't a soldier.
Garret covered him.
Bullets slammed into the ground.
Jayo flew through the air.
Traitors charged at him.
Jayo aimed.
He fired.
He missed.
He fired again.
Chests exploded.
Skulls shattered.
He hated killing.
Jayo charged.
Passing fighter plane after fighter.
Gunship after gunship.
Jayo's eyes narrowed.
He kept charging.
There was a gunship open.
Jayo turned.
Looking at the entrance of the hangar.
Fighters were incoming.
They fired.
Jayo fired.
Fighters exploded around him.
Jayo was thrown against the wall.
His back screamed in pain.
Adrenaline filled him.
The fighters fired.
Jayo screamed.
He ran.

He made it to the gunship.

Jayo climbed aboard.

A hand grabbed him.

Jayo spun.

He fired.

A traitor's corpse hit the deck.

The gunship activated.

Garret jumped onboard.

He flew to the controls.

Garret did something.

The shields activated.

The fighters fired.

Nothing happened.

Jayo aimed.

He fired.

The fighters exploded.

Chunks of smouldering wreckage covered the hangar.

The gunship flew away.

CHAPTER 14

Captain Garret shot the controls of the gunship and walked outside breathing in the fresh wonderful of Dragnic. He hadn't realised he'd missed fresh air until his time in the prison cell.

Holding his gun tightly in his hand, Garret focused on the massive bright orange plane of sandstone as he wondered about his next move. He was a soldier which only meant he followed orders but he didn't have any. He hated that.

Feeling the sandstone being crushed under his armoured leg, Garret wasn't sure what to do next. He would fight the traitors that was a certainty, Garret just had no idea how to do it.

Listening to the quiet howling wind that gently kicked sand into the air, Garret looked over at his beautiful Jayo who was sitting on the sandstone with his face in his hands.

Garret tried to smile as he remembered the first time he had killed a fellow human. It was years ago when the traitors first revealed themselves. Garret shook his head as he remembered the simple fight between his friends and the traitors. So many great warriors dead.

But Garret knew he would never forget the smooth squarish face of that traitor soldier. He would never forget blasting the brains of his own brother.

Every day he hated himself a tiny bit for killing his brother but it's what the Emperor would have wanted, and Garret had to protect the Human Empire. That was hard enough but he didn't love his brother. His love ended the moment he betrayed Garret.

Slowly walking over to Jayo and sitting next to him, Garret realised talking and comforting people wasn't his strong suit. If people gave Garret a gun, a knife or any weapon, he would be amazing. But Garret knew for a fact he was useless at truly comforting people.

Feeling Jayo press his warm, beautiful body against Garret, Garret tried to think about where to start.

"I remember my first kill," he said.

Jayo was silent.

"It was my brother. No one knows that. He turned traitor a few years back,"

Jayo looked up at Garret and frowned. "I'm... I'm sorry to hear that. I shouldn't be-"

Garret placed a soft finger on Jayo's lips. "You should be feeling how you are. I'll be scared if you didn't feel bad because of it. Killing is never easy,"

"How do you do it?"

Garret gave a light laugh. "I believe that every life I take helps protects humanity. Every kill protects people like my mum and dad,"

"Where are they?"

"I… don't know. They don't speak to me,"

Jayo nodded. "Mine don't speak to me because I'm gay. I know how it feels,"

Garret pressed his forehead against Jayo's. "I will protect you I promise,"

Jayo smiled. "I can protect myself,"

"I don't doubt that but the traitors will come,"

Jayo's smile went away and he nodded pulling away. Garret wanted to kick himself for that. Him and his big mouth ruining more moments.

"What's the plan, Professor? This is your wheelhouse," Garret asked.

Jayo crushed some of the sandstone in his hands.

"I'm not sure. We know the traitors are after the dragons and they want to control them,"

"Yes of course,"

Jayo leant close to Garret's ears. Garret felt like a schoolboy again as he felt Jayo's breath on his ear.

"I think they're after me,"

Garret pulled away.

"Why?"

Jayo showed Garret his hand. Garret shook his head when he didn't see anything. But after a few seconds Garret cocked his head as he saw a small blue glowing thing in Jayo's hand.

"What is it?"

"I don't know. I got it the first time I touched the dragon. It's how I calmed the other one down earlier,"

Garret nodded. "Can you control them?"

"I think so. The history books made reference to a device or being that could influence the dragons. But I always, always believed they were metaphorical in nature and not literal,"

"How would you interpret these books of yours if the references were literal?"

Jayo shrugged. "I don't know but… what if I could summon one?"

Garret was about to say something but his eyebrows rose when he saw Jayo's hand glow brighter.

"I think the glowing thing wants you to try," Garret said, he had no idea whatsoever how Jayo would do it.

Seeing Jayo close his eyes and raise the blue glowing thing in his hand close to his mouth, Garret held Jayo closer. He wasn't going to let anything happen to him.

"Dragon, we need you. We want to keep you safe. We want to protect you and our species. Please help us," Jayo said.

Looking around Garret couldn't see anything new. All he saw were the same miles upon miles of orange sandstone as earlier.

Resting his chin on Jayo's head, he could feel Jayo's body dropped as did his spirits. Garret wanted to know how to make Jayo feel better but he didn't know what it was like to be Jayo. Maybe the beautiful professor wanted the glowing thing to work, Garret nodded slightly as he realised that would be a great addition to a history book.

"What do you want to do now?" Jayo asked.

Garret tried not to smile. There were lots of creative things he wanted to do but he sadly knew what Jayo was talking about.

Garret looked into Jayo's beautiful eyes.

"What about that *much larger temple* you said about earlier?"

Jayo's eyes widened in delight. "Yes. We should go there. We should…"

The sound of massive heavy flapping wings filled the air and Garret's mouth dropped as he saw an immense golden dragon land tens of metres ahead of them.

Out of pure instinct, Garret held Jayo close but Jayo broke free and walked towards the dragon. Garret followed.

As they both walked towards the dragon, Garret was amazed by its beauty. The other dragons weren't as stunning or amazing as this one. Garret stared at the wonderous golden metallic scales on the creature. They shone bright in the early morning sun.

It was beautiful. Not Jayo beautiful but still pretty great.

The closer they got to the dragon, the more confident and alert Garret felt. He couldn't explain it but he felt alive and great.

The dragon lowered its head and smiled at them. Garret felt a little unnerved at the sight of all those metallic dagger-like teeth and those robotic golden eyes.

The dragon spoke. "Professor, we are not dragons. We. Are the Ancient Ones,"

CHAPTER 15

Professor Jayo watched in amazement as the stunning golden dragon raised its head. Jayo tried to absorb all the little details of its amazing glowing golden scales. Jayo could only start to understand how the metallic scales were formed and looked so perfect and shiny after three million years.

But what amazed him even more was Jayo noticed the massive dragon that looked like it weighed over a hundred tonnes, didn't crack the orange sandstone ground. The dragon didn't even make it crumble.

Looking at his own booted feet, Jayo's eyebrows rose when he saw two large dents in the sandstone from his own feet. How could a dragon weigh less than a human? Jayo didn't understand it.

Jayo took a step forward when he started to smell faint hints of burnt ozone and burnt wires. The smell reminded him of his times on a badly maintained transport shuttle years ago.

Staring at the dragon, Jayo wanted to learn more and he felt like this was his chance. He took another step towards the dragon at the sound of little motors whirring and humming inside. Jayo nodded as he felt like he was starting to scratch the surface of how the dragons worked. But there were still so many questions he wanted to ask and answered.

Feeling a wonderful body warmth near him, Jayo smiled as he knew his gorgeous Garret was standing firmly behind him. Jayo badly wanted to hold his hand and show he was strong against danger.

Jayo couldn't begin to imagine how Garret felt about the dragon. After all, Garret was a gorgeous warrior, a soldier moulded in the Emperor's image. And Jayo was only a professor, a professional historical investigator some might say. Their views and background hardly seemed like a match., but Jayo didn't care. He still wanted Garret.

Holding his cold grey metal trowel for comfort, Jayo stood firm as the dragon whirled its massive serpent like head around and lowered it in front of Jayo.

Jayo stared into those amazing bright red eyes, he was amazed by them. He knew they were machines and robotics but they looked so real, so amazing.

He remembered the history books mentioned their eyes were cold and distant and deadly. Jayo couldn't disagree more. They were stunning.

Then Jayo remembered what the dragon had said about them being known as the Ancient Ones. Jayo nodded as he recalled one weird reference to the Ancient Ones in the earliest textbook on the dragons. Everyone thought the Ancient Ones were their gods, Jayo had no idea the Ancient Ones were the dragons.

"Thank you for coming, *Ancient One*,"

The Dragon looked like it was narrowing its eyes but Jayo wasn't sure.

"You said you needed help Professor. We always come for the Chosen,"

Now the dragon was speaking, Jayo couldn't believe how angelic, softly spoke and wise the dragon sounded. He expected it to sound terrifying but he found the dragon oddly comforting.

"The Chosen?" Garret asked.

"Yes, it was foretold The Sleep would be ended by the touch of a Chosen. A worthy soul who in our culture was destined to destroy us or destroy an Empire,"

Jayo felt Garret step closer. "But I don't want to destroy anything, what's *The Sleep*?"

The dragon gave a sort of loud mechanical laugh. Jayo's fingers touched Garret.

"Your Emperor. He really didn't make us common knowledge, I guess that is what the Founders agreed with him those three million years ago,"

Jayo's and Garret's mouths dropped.

"Ha, humans. There is lots you don't know about your Emperor but he is the best human, best living creature I have ever met. Protect him at all costs,"

Jayo saw Garret nodding fiercely.

"What's The Sleep though?" Jayo asked.

The dragon bowed his head. "Three million years ago, there was a war. An alien race. We won the war but we were harmed too badly. Then we met the Emperor,"

Jayo's mind tried to understand it all. The dragon was creating more questions than answers. It was amazing and Jayo's eyes widened as he tried to remember all the details. He needed it for his history book. Jayo's stomach was filled with butterflies at the idea.

"The Emperor suggested we come to Dragnic and there were millions of sleep chambers for all of us. The Emperor spoke to our... you would call them Dragon Council. There was a bargain struck and the Ancient Ones entered a Sleep,"

Jayo's eyes narrowed. "What sort of bargain?"

"Professor, I do not know. I was not, I think you would say, present enough to know that information. But I saw the Emperor was extremely happy with what happened,"

Jayo nodded. He didn't know whether he was more amazed and excited about he was talking to a dragon or that he was talking to someone who had seen the Emperor in the flesh.

Garret stepped forward. "Why do the traitors want you? And did the Emperor want to know how to control you?"

The dragon shook his head. "No little soldier, the

Emperor definitely didn't want that. That was the purpose of the Sleep, he needed to allow time for our programming to reboot,"

Jayo raised his hand as the dragon's head rested on the ground. Black blood started to fill his eyes.

"So many of my friends fell during the War with the aliens. The aliens controlled them. We had to fix the error in our programming,"

Garret placed his arm around Jayo's shoulder.

"Please help us. Where can you be controlled from? We promise you we will stop the traitors if you tell us," Garrett said.

The dragon stared at Jayo and opened its massive jaw. Jayo stared into it but he wasn't afraid. He knew the dragon had to be testing him.

"I promise we will help you. Let your Ancient Ones sleep for another three million years. Just help us now," Jayo said.

The dragon nodded. "Fine, Professor. You are the Chosen and I will help you. Just know if you lie to me and give me to the traitors. There will be hell to pay,"

Jayo nodded. "That wouldn't be happening,"

He didn't know if he could keep that promise, he was only a professor after all. He wasn't a warrior but he hoped he could. Jayo really hoped.

"Human, we need to get to the space hulk there's a room-"

"With a strange black cube in it," Garret said.

The dragon smiled. "Yes, there's a thing in there

that we need. It will guide you to the Control Room. I don't remember after three million years,"

The sound of gunships roared towards them.

Jayo turned.

Ten grey gunships flew towards them.

Jayo rolled his eyes.

"We need a shuttle," Garret said.

The dragon whipped out its wings.

It roared.

Unleashing a torrent of fire.

"I haven't flown for three million years. Jump aboard humans!"

Jayo jumped on the dragon.

Hanging on its scales.

Oxygen filled his mouth.

The enemy fired.

The dragon flew.

Garret jumped on.

The dragon zoomed away.

CHAPTER 16

Captain Garret took a deep oxygen filled breath as the *interesting* golden dragon landed in a massive dirty grey metal hangar. Garret gagged at the thick smell of bleach badly hiding the smell of rotten flesh. Oddly enough making the taste of freshly roasted chicken form in his mouth.

Climbing off the dragon, Garret scanned the hangar carefully with his black metal gun. He wasn't going to be caught off guard, especially with his beautiful Jayo close by. Just the idea of him getting hurt made Garret's stomach tighten.

Feeling the cold grey metal floor under his armoured feet, Garret walked into the hangar a little more (and tried to avoid the metal crates that hazardously littered the hangar) as he heard the space hulk bang, pop and snap in the distance.

He couldn't quite place the noise but space hulks were weird things. Garret knew it was probably one of the reasons why he hated them so much. Most of them were just freaky and Garret shuddered at the memory of some of the things he had found in space hulks. It was never a good idea to explore a hulk made up of thousands of ships crushed together.

Hearing Jayo hop off the dragon, Garret tried to keep an eye on that beautiful man as Jayo seemed completely absorbed into the ship. Garret shook his head as he imagined Jayo ragging off the entire history of the production of the hangar in his mind.

Garret had no idea how someone found the history of hangars and ships interesting, but it made Jayo happy so Garret hardly minded.

Looking towards the massive metal hangar doors on the far side, Garret's eyes narrowed as he noticed they were open. He tried to remember what him and his team did yesterday.

Garret cocked his head as he realised they teleported off yesterday, so where was their shuttle? They came on one to the space hulk to complete their mission but it was missing now.

If there weren't traitors in the mix, Garret might have dismissed that and put it down to the Master of the Ship sending a team to retrieve it. But there were traitors in the mix. There were superhuman traitors.

Garret's eyes widened as he remembered the gunships didn't chase them into space. They didn't chase them at all. That alone was weird enough. It was almost like-

"Get down!" Garret shouted.

Bullets screamed through the air.

Exploding on the metal walls.
Chunks of metal flew off.
The dragon roared.
Black armoured superhumans charged out.
Garret whipped out his gun.
He fired.
He ran.
Jumping behind some metal crates.
Bullets slammed into them.
Jayo hissed.
Garret panicked.
He had to protect Jayo.
More bullets slammed into the crates.
A crate snapped.
Shards flew towards Garret.
He rolled forward.
The traitors saw him.
Garrct ran.
The dragon roared.
Unleashing a torrent of fire.
The traitors screamed.
They were burning.
Garret paused.
Bullets screamed towards him.
Superhumans flew at him.
They whacked him.
Garret went down.
He flew away.
A traitor grabbed him.
Smashing his fists into Garret.

Garret's vision blurred.
The traitors head disappeared.
Blood sprayed up Garret's face.
The dragon munched on the head.
The traitor fired.
Garret didn't stop.
He charged over to Jayo.
Tackling him to the ground.
Pulling Jayo behind some crates.
The traitors stormed at them.
They kept firing.
Garret couldn't find an opening.
The dragon roared.
An endless torrent shot out.
Garret looked up.
The traitors backed away.
Garret felt relieved.
Jayo punched his shoulder.
Garret looked up.
His eyes widened.
Five traitors were charging out.
Holding rocket launchers.
They aimed.
Garret tried to warn the dragon.
The traitors fired.
Garret grabbed Jayo.
Covering his eyes and ears.
The rockets smashed into the dragon.
Golden scales shattered.
Golden shards flew through the air.

Ripping into walls and crates.

Garret hissed.

A shard sliced into his armour.

He hugged Jayo tight.

A shard sliced through his hand.

Garret screamed.

The dragon collapsed.

Garret jumped up.

Whipping out his gun.

Shooting the traitors dead.

Looking at his hand, Garret bit his lip as he saw a massive splash of blood gush out. He forced himself to stay positive and think that at least he saved his beautiful Jayo's head. The shard would have killed him without his hand being there.

Garret felt two warm soft lips kiss his cheek. He smiled and turned to do more… but he frowned when he saw Jayo was already walking over to the dragon.

Garret rolled his eyes and smiled. At least he got a sort of kiss from Jayo, he did deserve it after all. He did just save Jayo's life.

Hearing the dragon's body hum and bang and sputter, Garret knelt next to Jayo as they both looked at the dying dragon.

"Chosen, this wasn't your war. You're a courageous one," the dragon said, forcing the words out.

Garret placed an arm around Jayo.

"Human, protect the Professor. You must go to

the cube room. Take this," the Dragon said, closing his eyes.

When he opened them, Garret almost shot back as he saw litres upon litres of dark thick black oil gush out of his left eye.

The solid red eye fell out into Jayo's hand. It pulsed bright red. Garret didn't know if this was touching or horrific.

"Go! Complete your mission, serve your Emperor," the dragon said.

Garret nodded knowing what the dragon meant.

He could see Jayo didn't want to leave the dragon just yet but as Garret looked out into the void. His eyes narrowed as he saw tens of gunships flew towards the space hulk.

"GO!" the dragon shouted.

The gunships fired.

Garret grabbed Jayo.

Jayo struggled.

The dragon rolled around.

Bullets smashed into the dragon.

The dragon roared a final time.

Unleashing a final bright purple torrent of fire.

Garret dragged Jayo.

They had to find the cube.

They had to stop the traitors.

CHAPTER 17

Professor Jayo's mouth dropped as he and his gorgeous Garret walked into the stunning black cube room. Jayo loved the look of it. It looked impressive and imposing, Jayo couldn't exactly place the room in history. That alone got him even more excited.

Focusing on the interesting rough-textured wall with their dark blue colour, Jayo's eyes focused as he tried to place the design. Jayo supposed he probably looked like an idiot but he was in his element. He loved exploring wrecks and placing in them in history.

After a few moments, Jayo frowned as he decided he couldn't place it in the history books. It didn't look human in actual fact, maybe alien. Jayo waved his hand as he realised that. He was far from an alien expert.

Smelling the odd lemony scent in the air, Jayo took a deeper breath and smelt something else. Burnt ozone. He nodded at that smell and turned to the blue metal pillar in the centre of the room.

Jayo gave the pillar a massive smile as he looked at it. It was utterly amazing, Jayo could only wonder how it got here. At first glance the smooth metal surface of the pillar didn't look right compared to the rough-textured walls. But it was still an impressive contrast.

Listening to the banging and creaking and popping of the space hulk, Jayo tried to force the idea of the traitors following them out of his mind. He really didn't want to think about them, but it did raise a question another day if the traitors did follow them. How would these massive superhumans travel through twisted narrow corridors? It was hard enough for a normal human.

Turning his attention to the pillar, Jayo lowered himself so he was eye-level with the target of their mission.

The black cube.

Jayo's eyes widened as he stared at this little amazing black cube just floating there above the pillar. He had heard great stories from friends about discoveries on alien ships about floating objects. Jayo smiled as he realised he should have listened more.

Focusing on the blue spheres that looked to be embedded into the cube, Jayo noticed the sphere pulse bright glowing blue as he got closer.

Jayo moved his hand down to his waist and placed it gently on his grey metal trowel in case he needed it. The blue sphere dulled a little. Jayo shook his head and grinned.

"My former squad wanted me to destroy it when we were last in here," Garret said, kneeling next to Jayo.

Jayo allowed his fingers to graze Garret's wounded hand that was thankfully healing. Jayo loved the sparks he felt between them.

"Thank you for not destroying it. Any details you remember from your first encounter?" Jayo asked.

"No, except when I told my squad I wasn't going to blow it up. The orbs pulsed,"

Jayo nodded and raised his hand to the cube. His hand and the spheres pulsed to one another. Jayo wondered if they were talking about something, but surely that couldn't be happening? Jayo shrugged. After today nothing surprised him.

An image of a massive sandstone cone filled his mind. Jayo tried to see where it was but he couldn't.

Jayo hissed.

He felt Garret hold him but Jayo could only see the massive cone in his mind. The pulsing of the sphere grew in intensity. Jayo held his head.

"What's going on?" Garret asked.

"I don't know. I can see another temple. It's massive,"

"The one you wanted to go to earlier,"

"No. Bigger. The temple. It feels dangerous, different,"

Jayo gasped as the image disappeared from his mind and saw the cube glowing bright blue.

Garret held Jayo and looked into his eyes. Jayo

looked back, he loved the look of Garret's deep blue eyes. They were so beautiful, so life filled and hopefully.

"Are you okay?" Garret asked.

Jayo was about to answer when he looked past Garret and saw blue markings on the rough walls. Jayo pushed away.

Standing up, Jayo's eyes narrowed as he studied each of the blue marks on the walls. They were being projected from the cube, Jayo wasn't really sure what they were but they looked like markings you might see on maps. Jayo smiled as he recognised some of the markings.

Garret pointed to the marking Jayo was looking at.

"Is that the destroyed temple we were at earlier?"

Jayo nodded. The symbol was faint but he recognised it as the symbol for a temple. Turning around, Jayo tried to find another one of the same symbols. Maybe this was the cube trying to show him where the control room was.

After a few moments, Jayo heard a strange clicking sound but Jayo dismissed it as just another sound of the space hulk. But Jayo pointed to a large blank space near the bottom of one of the walls.

"Why's it blank?" Garret asked.

"Garret, how best to hide information you never want to get out," Jayo said, holding out his hand to the blank space. Jayo bit his lip as he felt his hand glowing intensely.

Garret grinned as they both saw a list of coordinates on the wall. Jayo heard the clicking again.

"The dragons must have guessed the cube might be found. They needed to make sure only the Chosen saw the location," Jayo said, filling with excitement.

Garret screamed.

Something threw him to the ground.

Garret spun.

Jayo rushed over.

He stopped.

A metal spider spun.

Jumping on Jayo.

It slashed his t-shirt.

Jayo grabbed it.

He slammed it against the floor.

He stomped on it.

The spider survived.

It jumped on Jayo.

Climbing up him.

Jayo tried to grab it.

The spider dodged.

It got to Jayo's throat.

It went to slice into him.

Garret fired.

The spider exploded.

Watching the little metal corpse of the spider smash onto the rough textured ground, Jayo frowned as he recognised it. He knew exactly what the clicking was now, he hated how the spider's small camera had taken pictures of their discovery (including the coordinates) and sent them to the traitors.

Jayo's and Garret's eyes widened as they realised they had given the traitors everything they needed to control the dragons, and slaughter the Human Empire.

CHAPTER 18

Captain Garret stared with wide eyes at the little smashed up corpse of the metal spider as he felt his stomach tighten into a knot. He couldn't believe what just happened, for a brief moment Garret had felt happy they were ahead of the traitors.

That was gone.

Forcing himself to look away from that stupid little spider, Garret frowned as he looked at the rough dark blue walls, he hated this box room. Maybe his squad mates were right, maybe he should have blown up the cube.

Garret took a deep breath and tried to calm down. His hands formed fists. He instantly felt bad as he looked at his beautiful Jayo, his eyes were wide and his face... scared.

Garret took a step back as he tried to remember what face he had pulled but he couldn't. He felt his spirit sink a little as Garret remembered a little dark secret of his.

The blackouts he had as a teenager when he got angry, the damage he did to his home. The blackouts were always for seconds, but that's all he needed.

Taking a few more steps away from his beautiful Jayo, Garret tried to take another calming breath but he hated it. He hated himself, the thought that he might have hurt or threatened Jayo was too painful. But Garret really hated the smell of burnt ozone.

The sounds of the space creeping and snapping in the distance made Garret tense, but he relaxed when he felt a warm soft hand grab his.

Garret's stomach tightened even more but for a completely different reason now. It was why he hated his brother for turning traitor, Garret had found a way to channel his aggression and stop his blackouts. Garret shook his head as he remembered his brother spiralling out of control before he announced himself as a traitor to the Emperor.

A small part of Garret wondered what if he hadn't controlled himself better when he got angry. Would he be a traitor?

Or worse, what if Garret could have saved his brother if he had paid attention to him?

Garret felt a warm smooth finger press against the bottom of his chin and raise it so Garret looked into Jayo's soft innocent eyes.

"Did I hurt you?" Garret asked, his voice unsure and scared by the answer.

"No. I've met enough soldiers in my time to know the ones who are angry. Blackouts?"

Garret nodded.

"My husband was abused as a child. Beaten as a teenager. He was so angry when I met him,"

Garret looked to the floor. He never wanted Jayo to know about his past, at least not this part.

"What I'm saying is I understand. I'm here for you," Jayo said.

Garret's eyes widened. He was utterly stunned by Jayo's words. He had had boyfriends before but none of them knew about his angry past, and he knew for a fact none of them would have reacted like this.

Jayo leant closer to Garret. Garret loved the feeling of their lips grazed each other.

Something slammed into the hulk.

The entire room jerked.

Jayo fell backwards.

Garret fell to the ground.

The hulk banged.

Metal snapped.

Standing up, Garret rolled his eyes as he knew the traitors were doing exactly what he would have done if he was them. If two people had outlived their usefulness and they were a threat to his plan, Garret would have bombed the space hulk.

Helping Jayo back up, Garret tried to think of an escape, it would be minutes before the bombing chomped its way through the hulk and became a threat to them this deep in the space hulk.

Jayo started to look at the rough dark blue walls.

"What are you looking for?" Garret asked.

"I don't know,"

Garret looked back at the narrow twisted corridor they came through but he could see the metal snap and twist in that direction.

Jayo took out the red glowing eye of the dragon and raised it. Garret didn't understand it but it looked like Jayo wanted the eye to be looking at the wall.

The hulk shook violently.

"What are you doing?"

Jayo didn't answer.

The hulk snapped and banged.

Garret covered his ears.

A crack appeared in the walls.

"Got it!" Jayo shouted. He put the eye away.

The wall closest to Jayo dissolved.

Revealing a tunnel.

The hulk banged.

It shook.

The cracks got bigger.

Garret grabbed Jayo.

They dived into the tunnel.

They kept running.

Garret didn't stop.

Garret couldn't see clearly.

He ran on instinct.

The hulk shook.

Jayo almost fell.

Garret caught him.

They charged.

Running down the tunnel.

There was a light ahead.
Garret sped up.
They exited the tunnels.
Something roared.
Garret turned.
Flames engulfed the tunnel.
Garret and Jayo looked around.
There was nothing more than a black room.
The smell of smoke was overpowering.
They had to escape.
The hulk crackled.
Garret saw something.
He knew where they were.
They were in an old escape pod chamber.
Garret didn't know if the pods worked.
Jayo grabbed him.
Pulling him to a black disc.
Garret struggled.
Jayo kept pulling.
Garret didn't want to move.
Jayo hit him.
Pain flooded him.
Jayo threw him into a small black metal pod.
Garret panicked.
Jayo hit the controls.
Fire ripped through the hulk.
Annihilating it.
The hulk exploded.
The pod shot out into space.
Falling to the planet below.

CHAPTER 19

Professor Jayo frowned as he stared at the location of the coordinates the space hulk had given him. He was hardly impressed with the traitors for obliterating such a beautiful chunk of history.

Jayo's frown deepened as he remembered the utter terror he went through as the escape pod fell to the planet below. Thank the Emperor he remembered how that particular model worked. And thank the Emperor the escape pods weren't alien technology!

Taking a deep sandy breath that stunk of sweat and blood, Jayo focused on the location. Jayo looked down from a small orange sandstone cliff at the massive cone below.

A part of Jayo wished he was a painter of times like this, the massive orange sandstone cone was so beautiful and spectacular. Jayo could have spent years trying to discover how it was formed and able to survive for millions of years, but he knew he wouldn't be able to scratch the surface let alone discover anything too amazing.

It didn't make Jayo feel any less amazed by the cone but the sounds of shouting and machines drilling irritated him.

His eyes narrowed on the thousands of black armoured humans with their pathetic guns and machines down below. Jayo wanted them all to stop and go home. This was a historical monument, he didn't want it destroyed or damaged. This drilling was an insult to history.

Outrageous!

Jayo rolled his eyes as he saw some of the foes below were much taller, larger and stronger than the other humans in black armour. He hated that there were superhuman traitors here.

Thinking of how to get to the cone-like temple, Jayo shrugged as he realised, they couldn't get to it. They wouldn't fight through the thousands of humans. That was suicide. They couldn't summon a dragon, that was foolish and-

Jayo turned to his gorgeous and utterly beautiful Garret who was focusing too much on the traitors to notice Jayo. For a moment Jayo considered saying something rude to see Garrett would react. But he was a professor, a man of (low) distinction, and sadly he wouldn't do that.

"Earth to Garret," Jayo said, running his fingers over Garret's rough body armour.

Garret didn't react.

Knowing full well Garret was too focused. Jayo

remembered for a moment how Garret had acted towards him in the room with the cube. It was like looking at his husband again, so traumatised, so beautiful, so amazing.

It took everything Jayo had not to confess his love for Garret in that moment, but he just wasn't ready. He really did care about Garrett but... Jayo wasn't sure if he was over his husband yet. The last thing he wanted was to get with Garret and realise he was only with him as a rebound from his husband.

That wasn't fair on Garret.

Trying not to think about that Jayo took out the massive red robotic eye and decided to do something strange. He held it out in front of him and stared through it.

Jayo was surprised that the eye seemed to know what he wanted to do because it kept getting clearer.

"What you doing now?" Garret asked.

"You were too busy so I wanted to do something by myself," Jayo said.

He smiled as the eye showed him something. It looked like there was a tunnel under the cone temple leading towards them.

Moving the eye around and following the run, Jayo gave a quiet laugh as the entrance looked to be twenty metres from them.

"Come on, I've found a shortcut," Jayo said, walking over to the entrance.

Looking at the piece of dark orange sandstone where the entrance should have been, Jayo cocked his head as he tried to decide what to do. He placed a hand on his grey metal trowel in case he needed to dig.

Garret kicked the sandstone.

Jayo went to moan at him but they both grinned as the sandstone crumbled, revealing a black hole the size of a fist.

Kneeling down, Jayo took out his grey metal trowel and stabbed the sandstone with it. Within moments, the sandstone crumbled away.

"Nice," Garret said, offering Jayo a hand down.

Jayo didn't hesitate. He took Garret's rough hands and tried not to smile as he felt the chemistry between them as Jayo helped him down into the tunnel.

Hearing Garret behind him, Jayo stared down the long perfectly smooth tunnel that headed straight for the dragon temple. Which Jayo hoped was the control centre for the dragons.

As they walked down the tunnel, Jayo was amazed at how smooth the tunnel's sandstone walls were, and he was even surprised that the walls were glowing faintly. Providing just enough light to see but not too much light to blind you.

An odd happy medium.

The smell of fresh clean air made Jayo smile a little in wonder as he tried to figure out why that was.

Perhaps the temple ahead was open to the escape and only looked like a sandstone cone from the outside. Jayo wasn't sure. It sounded far fetched but if that wasn't correct then Jayo had no clue how the air in the tunnel wasn't stale and foul.

After a few minutes of walking, Jayo saw daylight ahead and he felt a hot breeze of fresh smelling air.

Looking at Garret, they both smiled at each other. Jayo loved the idea that their mission was almost done, he would have more than enough material to maybe write a new history book and show everyone the dragons were real, and maybe, just maybe he could be with Garret.

Jayo stupidly allowed a small voice inside his head to laugh at him. A part of Jayo doubted his dreams with Garret would ever happen.

Garret was a military man, a man of action, he wouldn't want to be with a professor. Garret would leave him the second Jayo's mission was over. Jayo hated that idea.

Jayo forced that little voice of doubt away. He was going to confess his love to Garret soon and he would (hopefully) prove his doubts wrong.

As they walked out of the tunnel, Jayo's mouth dropped at the sight of the control centre.

It was stunning.

CHAPTER 20

Captain Garret allowed a small smile to show on his smooth face as he and his beautiful Jayo walked into the control centre of the dragons.

Garret stared in amazement at the smooth bronze dome that shone bright as light shone through the opening in the very top of the dome.

He couldn't believe the control centre was inside a massive sandstone cone. It seemed so simple, too perfect for such an advanced enemy. But after years of service to the Emperor, Garret wasn't surprised by too much anymore.

The shining dragon heads high above him embedded in the bronze dome made Garret cover his eyes and look away. He felt the hot light warm his skin and a drop of sweat ran down his back.

At least with him knowing there was an opening in the centre, it told Garret why the air was so fresh and clean in the tunnel. Even breathing in this air, Garret was glad to still have fresh, sweet smelling air.

The sound of Jayo tapping the bronze with his grey metal trowel made Garret's eyes narrowed as he tried to figure out what the stunning man was doing.

Then Garret focused on what Jayo was tapping and chipping away at. Garret cocked his head as he saw a large red sandstone dome in the centre with a flat top.

He remembered the hologram from yesterday that showed them the map of the planet but that wasn't red. Maybe the dragons or even the amazing Emperor himself had tried to put people off uncovering the sandstone. Red was the colour of danger after all.

Attempting to think more logical than that, Garret walked over to the dome and ran his fingers over its rough red surface. Some of the sandstone crumbled away but it turned into fine dust that smelt of burnt rubber.

Garret turned to Jayo who was kneeling on the ground next to him tapping away at the sandstone, and instead of asking what he thought of the dome. Garret felt a wave of confidence wash over him. It wasn't logical but Garret really wanted to tell Jayo how he felt.

The sandstone crumbled away. As did Garret's moment and confidence.

Revealing a massive black table with lights flashing all over it, Garret gave Jayo a fake smile as Jayo jumped up and down.

A red flashing light on the other side of the table

caught both of their attention. Walking over to it, Garret and Jayo looked puzzled at each other. There was a large slot in the table the size of a bowling ball.

Garret smiled as he knew the answer before the Professor.

"Try your eye thing," he said.

Jayo smiled and carefully placed the large mechanical red eye inside the slot. The sound of humming and shrieking filled the control centre for a few moments before everything went silent.

"Is that meant to happen?" Garret asked.

Jayo shrugged. "I don't know. There was never any mention of the control centre in the books,"

Garret tapped the table a few times. The table slowly hummed again and a pentagram of a holographic projector raised off the table. They didn't show anything.

Seeing Jayo rolled his eyes, he held out his hand and Garret saw it glow bright blue at the table.

After a few seconds, the projectors hummed to life. Revealing thousands of streams of data and information, there was no chance Garret could or would process it all.

Then lots of the streams got pushed out by a massive yellow hologram of the planet with each stream of data pointing to a particular location as the planet spun.

Garret looked at Jayo. He had no idea what this was.

"Any ideas?"

Jayo pointed to the holographic planet. "Look how each of the streams is specific to each location. I think they're dormant dragons,"

Garret nodded. "That makes sense. So this is definitely the control centre. How do you stop them from activating now?"

Jayo shook his head. "My question is where are the other awaken dragons? Remember there were three of them earlier and none of them were the golden one,"

"True," Garret said, clapping his hands.

"What are you doing?"

"I'm making the map do something. I just clap my hands in my quarters on the Emperor's Fist and the lights turn on and off,"

Jayo placed his face in his hands. Garret was hopeless.

"Do you have a better idea?" Garret asked.

"No," Jayo said.

"Wait, try your Chosen thing in your hand,"

Garret saw Jayo stare at his hand as he held it up and Garret's eyes narrowed as he saw it pulse. Maybe it was pulsing with each thought of Jayo. Garret wasn't sure but he would love to know the answer.

Slowly the hologram flashed a few times and the thousands of streams of data went away. Leaving only four streams of data all in the far, far north of Dragnic.

Garret smiled. "That's impressive,"

"It is bad if I said I didn't want to keep them

asleep,"

"No, this is great. Do something else," Garret said, he knew it wasn't a toy but they needed to learn how to use the controls before stopping the traitors from controlling them.

Jayo shook his head. "You know we can't,"

"Fine, what command are you going to enter?"

Garret saw the look of uncertainty in Jayo's eyes and how Jayo hunched over. He had seen that look before, the feeling like the fate of millions rested on your shoulders. Garret hated that feeling but he knew it all too well.

He walked over to Jayo and placed his arms tightly around him. Garret wasn't going to let him think he was alone, Garret had had that feeling too many times when he had felt the same. No one should ever have to feel alone when the lives of millions are in your hands.

"Show up the control functions," Jayo said.

The holograph flashed and tens of streams of data showed up but Garret didn't recognise any of the language in there. Meaning of course Jayo knew what he was looking at.

Bullets slammed into Garret's back.

They flew through him.

Blood covered his hands.

He dropped to the ground.

CHAPTER 21

Professor Jayo screamed as he felt the bullets slam into his gorgeous Garret and Garret's body went limp.

Jayo turned around and caught the love of his life. Lowering him down carefully so he was pressed against the holographic table. Jayo stared into those deep, rich beautiful eyes.

The black holographic table flashed as Garret's blood coated its metal sides. Jayo wanted to apologise using the thing in his hand but he didn't care.

He only cared that Garret was okay.

Jayo's eyes narrowed and his hands formed fists as five black armoured superhuman traitors walked in. Their bodies tall and larger than a normal human. They were disgusting!

How dare they attack Garret!

Jayo tried to calm down but he was furious at these traitors. Then he remembered he was in control here. The control centre responded to him and (hopefully) only him.

Taking a deep breath of the wonderfully fresh, sweet-smelling air, Jayo's eyes narrowed on the truly disgusting traitors as they marched into the centre.

Jayo hated the long white robes of the Master of the Ship with his ugly gaunt features and pathetic face. The only thing Jayo wanted to do was attack and… he didn't know. Jayo wasn't a fighter.

The twisted, crackling laugh of The Herald of The End filled the centre as he marched in. His gun still smoking. How dare that idiot shoot Garret.

Jayo's fists tightened as he fought the want to smash his fists into the Herald's twisted, sliced up face. Which still included the half destroyed face of Jayo's husband.

Jayo would kill him that was a promise.

"Mortal, you are a gift to the traitors. Because of your amazing actions, the Human Empire will fall!" the Herald shouted.

Jayo spat at him.

"Show some respect!" the Master shouted.

The Herald slapped him. "Be silent. He is a guest. He has made it possible. What did you do Master?"

The Master's eyes widened. "I did everything! I found this planet. I found the professor. I-"

The Herald grabbed his skull.

Jayo placed his hand on his chest and he tried to block the memories of seeing his husband die.

"You! Have outlived your usefulness,"

The Herald shattered his skull. The Master's body fell to the ground.

The herald smiled and licked his armoured fingers as he walked over to Jayo. Jayo wanted to run away but he couldn't. His legs wouldn't move and Jayo hated how close the Herald was to him.

"Beautiful, isn't it Mortal?"

Jayo stayed silent.

"You will tell me what I want to know, Mortal. So many try to resist. So many die,"

"Did my husband resist?"

The Herald smiled. "Self-defence I'll say. And he deserved it. All those who serve the Emperor must die,"

The Herald kicked Garret in the ribs. Garret hissed.

"Enough," Jayo said. "What do you want?"

"Tell me how it works, Mortal,"

Jayo laughed. "Never. I will not let you kill millions,"

The Herald cocked his head. "Mortal, I don't want to kill millions. I want to enslave trillions. I want the Empire to be mine,"

"You seriously think you can do that with some dragons," Jayo said.

His hand burnt.

Jayo fell to the floor.

He screamed.

His hand glowed bright blue.

It was burning him.

"I was trying to protect you," Jayo said, tears streaming down his face.

The Herald walked over to him, smiling.

"Dragons. So prideful,"

The Herald gripped Jayo's hand. He screamed as he felt his bones being crushed.

"Bring me the knife," the Herald said.

Jayo's eyes widened as a large red hot blade was passed to the Herald.

"This won't hurt a bit,"

Jayo's hand glowed bright blue in protest.

The Herald swung.

Jayo screamed in agony. Crippling pain filled him.

Laying on the cold sandstone ground, Jayo screamed as he looked at his arm. The bastard sliced it from the forearm.

Jayo tried to think but the pain was crippling. He hated the Herald.

The Herald chomped on Jayo's arm. Then he smiled and his eyes glowed bright blue. Jayo's stomach twisted into a tight knot.

"That foolish Master Mortal doubted my plan. He said I should have hunted you from the start. I was right, he was just another foolish mortal. You have done your purpose so well,"

Jayo tried to will his body to calm down and fight. Wave after wave of searing pain flooded his body.

Jayo screamed.

The Herald shook his head at Garrett. "You see here soldier, look as I launch the death of your Empire. I am the Herald of the End,"

Jayo forced himself to look at Garret.

Another wave of crippling pain.

Garret wasn't moving. He stared at the Herald.

Jayo knew he had to-

A wave of searing pain flooded his head.

Jayo knew he had to stop this. He couldn't imagine what surviving a failure this massive would do to Garret.

Jayo had to find his courage, but he was a professor. He was an arm down.

The Herald stared at the hologram above the table, his eyes bright blue and glaring at the planet. Jayo hated this.

"Stop!" Jayo shouted. "Ancient Ones fight this Herald. I am the Chosen. I. Will. Protect You,"

The Herald laughed. "No you won't"

He kicked Jayo in the head.

Slicing deep.

Blood ran down Jayo's face.

Garret screamed. He tried to move. He couldn't.

The Herald shook his head. Jayo moved to snap that idiot's head.

"Mortals, your time is done.," the Herald said, staring into the hologram. "Wake them all!"

Jayo opened his mouth to scream but his body went weak. He knew he had failed as he watched the streams of data flash and change colour.

This wasn't happening. Jayo had to stop this. He wasn't going to let his Empire burn. So much history would die. So many people would die. His Garret would die.

Jayo found his courage.

He jumped up.

Screaming.

He charged.

He leapt on the Herald.

The superhuman traitors flew at Jayo.

Jayo slammed his fists into the Herald.

He moaned.

Jayo kept smashing.

He slashed the Herald.

Ripping off his husband's face.

Hands grabbed him.

The Herald whacked Jayo round the face.

Feeling the traitors hold him, Jayo tried to struggle but he knew it was useless. The traitors were holding him with superhuman strength. The Herald smiled at Jayo.

"Brave Mortal. Stupid but brave. If I had access to the equipment, I would have you sent to the mind camps. You would be useful to the traitors,"

Garret moaned and tried to shout at that idea.

"Ignore him, Mortal. Look at the hologram,"

Jayo kept blinking as the searing pain returned to him. He tried to focus on the hologram. His eyes widened as he saw thousands of dragons being released from their Sleep,"

Without knowing why, Jayo stared at the Herald. Imaging his head being chomped off by a dragon and he whispered a simple phrase but he knew in that moment he wasn't just a professor.

He was a professor who would happily die protecting the man he loved.

"Fight this and I will protect you," Jayo said.

The Herald gripped his chin. "What did you say!"

Jayo smiled. "I said *fight this*!"

The Herald screamed.

His eyes glowed.

Blinding everyone.

The superhumans screamed in agony.

Jayo kicked them.

Adrenaline filled his body.

He punched them.

Grabbing a gun.

He fired,

He still hated it.

He needed to defend himself.

Jayo fired again and again.

The superhumans were dead.

The Herald whacked Jayo.

The gun flew away.

Jayo charged.

The Herald punched.

He kicked.

Jayo blocked them.

He remembered fighting books.

Jayo slammed his fists into the Herald.

The Herald laughed.

Jayo jumped into the air.

He kicked the Herald in the head.

The Herald slammed on the floor.

He looked dead.

Jayo walked up. Looking at the herald. He got too close.

The Herald leapt forward.

Knocking Jayo over.

The Herald grabbed Jayo's skull.

He raised the skull.

Jayo screamed.

A gun roared.

The Herald's head exploded.

Garret collapsed to the ground. A smoking gun in his hand.

Jayo wanted to help.

He had to save the Empire.

He had to be Garret in that moment.

Jayo looked at the hologram.

Thousands of dragons were flying into space.

He had to stop them.

Jayo grabbed the Herald's corpse.

His fingers searched the shattered skull.

As soon as Jayo saw a small blue glowing piece of flesh in amongst all the shattered brain matter, Jayo relaxed and smiled.

Holding the glowing piece of flesh, Jayo closed his eyes and held it out to the hologram.

"Listen carefully, as your Chosen I command you

to destroy the Emperor's Fist and send a simple message I'll give you in a moment. Then you will all return to Sleep for another ten million years. I will protect you,"

Jayo had no idea if the hologram and dragons would listen to him, but as he opened up his hands he saw the piece of flesh pulse dimly before going out.

He couldn't quite describe the feeling but it felt as if something beautiful had just died in his hands.

Looking back at the hologram, it flashed and Jayo smiled as he saw the wreckage of the Emperor's Fist plummeting to Dragnic, along with thousands of Dragons returning to the planet with it.

"Destination? Message?" a computerised voice asked.

"Send it to Earth. The Message is *The Three Million Years Ago Secret is aSleep,*"

The hologram flashed a final time before going out and Jayo's eyes widened as he saw a thick layer of orange sandstone formed around the holographic table.

Jayo looked over at his beautiful Garret who smiled at him. Jayo smiled back. Their mission was done. It was over.

CHAPTER 22

Captain Garret laid on a wonderfully soft white sheet on a sterile white hospital bed aboard the *Victor's Medic* in high orbit of Dragnic.

He didn't know why he was so surprised the ships came so quickly but he was. Garret thought they would come within days not hours.

But as he allowed the soft sheets to take the full weight of his body, Garret was glad they had come. Especially as he looked at his battered muscular body with a massive white sheet of cloth wrapped around his chest.

Garret smiled as he remembered the shocked look at the doctor's face when she saw the bullet wounds and he was still alive.

Barely, but alive.

As Garret stared up at the sterile white ceiling of the little medical box room, he finally realised the true extent of his feelings for Jayo.

In all honesty, Garret knew for a hundred

percent certainty he didn't stay alive for the Empire, Emperor or his duty. He stayed alive to protect Jayo because the thought of losing the love of his life was too hard to think about.

He might have failed Saraho and let her die. But Garret swore he would protect Jayo and that's what he did.

The sounds of the medical equipment either side of him bleak and hum quietly made Garret just want to get out of here and see Jayo. Thank him for everything and confess his love for him.

He wanted Jayo more than anything he had known that before but being shot clarified that for him. He couldn't imagine or want a life without Jayo.

There was just something about him. His mind, his knowledge, his endless ability to surprise Garret (he had no idea Jayo could fight) there was just something amazing about Jayo. Something Garret wanted to explore and love for a long, long time.

The smell of medical grade bleach with a disgusting hint of lemon added to Garret's determination to see (and love) Jayo. But he supposed he better wait for a few minutes for the doctor to get back.

Pressing his head into the soft pillow, Garret wondered what if the Emperor was a divine being like some weird cults suggested. Would he be proud of Garret?

Garret grinned and shook his head. It didn't matter to him. After all these years of service to the

Emperor, Garret only now realised he did love the Empire and wanted to protect it with all his might.

But he needed to stop chasing some idea in the back of his mind that the Emperor would thank him personally at some point.

Taking a deep bleach-filled breath, Garret nodded to himself as he remembered what one of the oaths he took when he first signed into the army. It was something along the lines of to serve is the reward in itself.

Garret couldn't agree more, on every mission he had wanted and been driven to serve and protect his Emperor, and he had on this mission too.

He wanted to kick himself for thinking himself as a failure on this mission. Sure Garret had made some mistakes but all the great war heroes did. It was a part of their war story so Garret gave a massive grin as it clicked.

He might actually be a great war hero one day because he served his Emperor and protect what the Emperor stood for in the face of impossible odds. And that him made damn proud to be a soldier.

Standing up, Garret pulled a bright white hospital robe over himself and he was going to wrap up his time on Dragnic properly.

He was going to confess his love for Jayo. No matter what interruptions happened. He loved Jayo and Jayo was going to know.

CHAPTER 23

Professor Jayo sat on a cold metal crate in the middle of the quiet hangar on the *Victor's Medic*. Listening to the quiet roar of the engines and the quiet talking of soldiers and doctors on the far side of the hangar.

Jayo looked around and happily admitted this had to be his favourite hangar in history. Its long reinforced white metal walls made it perfect for repelling attacks, and its improved ventilation definitely made the air smell better.

Breathing in the air, Jayo loved the fresh sweet smell of it. That sweet smell reminded Jayo of the delicious sugar pies his grandfather use to make back on his homeworld. There was something so refreshing and almost reinvigorating about the smell. Jayo was sure it had something to do with almost dying. But it was still true.

Staring out through the shielded entrance into space, Jayo couldn't help but smile as he stared out on the massive orange planet known as Dragnic.

Jayo had come here after being disgraced with his career in shreds of its former glory all because he wanted to prove the dragons were real. He was right they were real.

But his smile lessened a little as he realised his career might not be as bright as it once was because everything relied on evidence. He didn't have any.

Jayo couldn't prove the history of the Sleep, that the Emperor was over three million years old and he couldn't prove the dragons were even real, unless he harmed one. Which Jayo refused to do.

Running his fingers over the cold metal of the crate, Jayo cocked his head as he remembered that he might have set out to try and build his career and he had. Jayo had been successful n that because he had more than enough material to write an epic saga of the true history of the dragons.

Whether or not it built his career... that didn't matter to Jayo anymore. He knew the truth and to him that was more important and special.

Jayo gave himself a large teenage boy smile as he knew he had found something far greater than a career on Dragnic. He had found his amazing, gorgeous, brilliant Garret.

Ever since his husband was slaughtered, Jayo actually didn't know if he would ever love another man again. But his amazing Garret proved him wrong and what amazed Jayo even more was Garret never argued, never questioned no matter how weird or wacky his ideas were. Garrett stood by him and was loyal.

There was something precious about that.

Standing up, Jayo stretched his back and neck and was about to leave to find his gorgeous Garret when a small pink disc floated towards him and it flashed.

Jayo knew what this was, he had heard of these message discs from friends who worked in the most secret departments of the Emperor's government on Earth. Jayo's eyes narrowed as he tried to think about what it was doing here.

He pressed it. A smooth, velvety voice with an edge of authority spoke to him.

"Dear Professor Jayo, I have been watching you and I want to thank you. I have written to your university and you are being requisitioned by a special but important division of the Emperor's government.

I have requisitioned Captain Garret too.

Please enjoy your stay on the Victor's Medic and I will be in contact with you soon about your new mission for the Emperor on Earth. You will love it, and tell Captain Garret he shall meet the Emperor all because of you.

Kind Regards,

Sarah Oddballa."

With that, the little disc flew away and Jayo sat back down on the cold metal crate behind him. He didn't know what to think about first- the weird message or the amazing new career he had found. Or the career found him.

He knew it sounded all too good to be true but Jayo was excited about this new adventure and next step in his life. He had heard amazing stories from his old friends that retired from their secret work and they loved it. Jayo knew he would too.

His stomach filled with butterflies at the idea of having everything he wanted. Jayo was going to write his epic saga of the true dragon history and he was going to build his career to its former glory. Even if his accomplishments were only known to a select few.

But there was something else he needed.

Turning around, Jayo went lightheaded a little as he watched his gorgeous Garret with his smooth face and amazing looks and his beautiful brown hair bun walk towards him.

Jayo didn't want to waste any more time and he didn't want to risk losing Garret not after everything they had been through.

Jayo ran over to him. And wrapped his arms around Garret, Jayo loved the chemistry and electricity between them.

Garret kissed Jayo and he didn't hesitate or pause. Jayo kissed right back loving the feeling of Garret's soft lips against his.

"I love you Garret,"

Garret smiled and gave Jayo another deep passionate kiss.

"I love you too. I don't want to waste any more time. I want to be with you,"

Jayo gave him a boyish grin and took off Garret's

hairband and run his fingers through Garret's stunning long brown hair.

"That's good because we are together. We have a new job together on Earth,"

Garret's eyes widened and he wrapped his arms around Jayo tightly. Walking off back towards their quarters, Jayo pressed his head against Garret's.

"How long until we get to Earth?" Garret asked.

"This model of transport... three and half months," Jayo said.

Giving Jayo another kiss, Garret said "A long time to get to know each other, and hopefully do a lot more,"

Jayo smiled and as he wrapped his arm around the man he loved. He knew the future was going to be great and bright. Jayo had survived the Herald of the End and with his gorgeous Garret by his side, he could do anything.

And that was a fact.

AUTHOR'S NOTE

Thanks for reading, I hope you enjoyed it.

Personally, I absolutely loved this book. I thought it was great fun to write from the two main characters to the planet to the dragons or the Ancient Ones.

For me, the entire point of the book was to introduce the Agents of The Emperor Series in novella form for the first time. Because I've done at least 30 short stories in the universe and loved it.

But I haven't done a longer story so this is why I wanted to write the book, and I really, really wanted to play around with the idea of space dragons!

And I didn't realise it at the time but this novella built upon the short story *The First Rememberer* who explores the start of the Human Empire and the Coming of the Emperor. That's a great short story!

Since that story really expanded the scope of the series with the Empire being over a hundred thousand years old and the main character in that story is that old. So he saw the Emperor.

But I never, ever expected the Emperor to be over three million years old that will be fun to explore in future books.

Personally, my favourite part of this book was the romance between Jayo and Garret because as I writing it. I too was getting annoyed that they kept going to kiss but something kept interrupting them. So I was really happy when the characters did actually kiss and get together.

That was definitely my favourite part to write.

I know this book is perfectly standalone but I'm not entirely sure if these characters will never pop up again. Mainly because now I'm interested in what their new job could be and who's Sarah Oddballa.

I explore her character a little bit in the Drake Science Fiction Private Eye Short Stories but we still don't know much about her.

Finally, I know I normally talk about my inspiration in these Author's Notes but I honestly don't know where I got my inspiration from this time. It was probably a combination of the books I've read, films I've watched and more.

Thanks again for reading and I hope to see you in another book soon.

Have a great day!

GET YOUR FREE EXCLUSIVE GARRO SHORT STORY HERE!

https://www.subscribepage.com/garrosignup

Thank you for reading.
I hoped you enjoyed it.
If you want a FREE book and keep up to date about new books and project. Then please sign up for my newsletter at
www.connorwhiteley.net/
Have a great day.

About the author:

Connor Whiteley is the author of over 30 books in the sci-fi fantasy, nonfiction psychology and books for writer's genre and he is a Human Branding Speaker and Consultant.

He is a passionate warhammer 40,000 reader, psychology student and author.

Who narrates his own audiobooks and he hosts The Psychology World Podcast.

All whilst studying Psychology at the University of Kent, England.

Also, he was a former Explorer Scout where he gave a speech to the Maltese President in August 2018 and he attended Prince Charles' 70th Birthday Party at Buckingham Palace in May 2018.

Plus, he is a self-confessed coffee lover!

OTHER SHORT STORIES BY CONNOR WHITELEY

Blade of The Emperor
Arbiter's Truth
The Bloodied Rose
Asmodia's Wrath
Heart of A Killer
Emissary of Blood
Computation of Battle
Old One's Wrath
Puppets and Masters
Ship of Plague
Interrogation
Sacrifice of the Soul
Heart of The Flesheater
Heart of The Regent
Heart of The Standing
Feline of The Lost
Heart of The Story
The Family Mailing Affair
Defining Criminality
The Martian Affair
A Cheating Affair
The Little Café Affair
Mountain of Death
Prisoner's Fight
Claws of Death

Bitter Air
Honey Hunt
Blade On A Train
City of Fire
Awaiting Death
Poison In The Candy Cane
Christmas Innocence
You Better Watch Out
Christmas Theft
Trouble In Christmas
Smell of The Lake
Problem In A Car
Theft, Past and Team

Other books by Connor Whiteley:

The Fireheart Fantasy Series
Heart of Fire
Heart of Lies
Heart of Prophecy
Heart of Bones
Heart of Fate

City of Assassins (Urban Fantasy)
City of Death

Agents of The Emperor
Return of The Ancient Ones

The Garro Series- Fantasy/Sci-fi
GARRO: GALAXY'S END
GARRO: RISE OF THE ORDER
GARRO: END TIMES
GARRO: SHORT STORIES
GARRO: COLLECTION
GARRO: HERESY
GARRO: FAITHLESS
GARRO: DESTROYER OF WORLDS
GARRO: COLLECTIONS BOOK 4-6
GARRO: MISTRESS OF BLOOD
GARRO: BEACON OF HOPE
GARRO: END OF DAYS

Winter Series- Fantasy Trilogy Books
WINTER'S COMING
WINTER'S HUNT
WINTER'S REVENGE
WINTER'S DISSENSION

Miscellaneous:
THE ANGEL OF RETURN
THE ANGEL OF FREEDOM

All books in 'An Introductory Series':
BIOLOGICAL PSYCHOLOGY 3RD EDITION
COGNITIVE PSYCHOLOGY THIRD EDITION
SOCIAL PSYCHOLOGY- 3RD EDITION
ABNORMAL PSYCHOLOGY 3RD EDITION
PSYCHOLOGY OF RELATIONSHIPS- 3RD EDITION
DEVELOPMENTAL PSYCHOLOGY 3RD EDITION
HEALTH PSYCHOLOGY
RESEARCH IN PSYCHOLOGY
A GUIDE TO MENTAL HEALTH AND TREATMENT AROUND THE WORLD- A GLOBAL LOOK AT DEPRESSION
FORENSIC PSYCHOLOGY
THE FORENSIC PSYCHOLOGY OF THEFT, BURGLARY AND OTHER RIMES AGAINST PROPERTY
CRIMINAL PROFILING: A FORENSIC PSYCHOLOGY GUIDE TO FBI PROFILING AND GEOGRAPHICAL AND STATISTICAL PROFILING.
CLINICAL PSYCHOLOGY
FORMULATION IN PSYCHOTHERAPY

PERSONALITY PSYCHOLOGY AND INDIVIDUAL DIFFERENCES
CLINICAL PSYCHOLOGY REFLECTIONS VOLUME 1
CLINICAL PSYCHOLOGY REFLECTIONS VOLUME 2
CULT PSYCHOLOGY
Police Psychology

Companion guides:
BIOLOGICAL PSYCHOLOGY 2ND EDITION WORKBOOK
COGNITIVE PSYCHOLOGY 2ND EDITION WORKBOOK
SOCIOCULTURAL PSYCHOLOGY 2ND EDITION WORKBOOK
ABNORMAL PSYCHOLOGY 2ND EDITION WORKBOOK
PSYCHOLOGY OF HUMAN RELATIONSHIPS 2ND EDITION WORKBOOK
HEALTH PSYCHOLOGY WORKBOOK
FORENSIC PSYCHOLOGY WORKBOOK

Audiobooks by Connor Whiteley:
BIOLOGICAL PSYCHOLOGY
COGNITIVE PSYCHOLOGY
SOCIOCULTURAL PSYCHOLOGY
ABNORMAL PSYCHOLOGY
PSYCHOLOGY OF HUMAN RELATIONSHIPS
HEALTH PSYCHOLOGY
DEVELOPMENTAL PSYCHOLOGY
RESEARCH IN PSYCHOLOGY
FORENSIC PSYCHOLOGY
GARRO: GALAXY'S END
GARRO: RISE OF THE ORDER
GARRO: SHORT STORIES
GARRO: END TIMES
GARRO: COLLECTION
GARRO: HERESY
GARRO: FAITHLESS
GARRO: DESTROYER OF WORLDS
GARRO: COLLECTION BOOKS 4-6
GARRO: COLLECTION BOOKS 1-6

Business books:

TIME MANAGEMENT: A GUIDE FOR STUDENTS AND WORKERS

LEADERSHIP: WHAT MAKES A GOOD LEADER? A GUIDE FOR STUDENTS AND WORKERS.

BUSINESS SKILLS: HOW TO SURVIVE THE BUSINESS WORLD? A GUIDE FOR STUDENTS, EMPLOYEES AND EMPLOYERS.

BUSINESS COLLECTION

GET YOUR FREE BOOK AT:
WWW.CONNORWHITELEY.NET

Lightning Source UK Ltd.
Milton Keynes UK
UKHW020941180522
403171UK00011B/1071